Sons of Heaven: The Haunted

By
Thomas Harwick

Dedication

This is dedicated to my family and friends who put up with, and even supported me while I chased my crazy dream; to the people, places, and experiences that inspired me, and to my God who strengthens me.

I can't get to everyone, that would take another book, but here are a few of the people that really helped me with the creation of this book.

First and foremost my three editors, and yes, I did just say THREE editors.

My grammar and spelling editor – My Mother

My form and style editor – Aunt Maggie

My technical editor – Uncle Jeff (by the way, did you guys know there is a difference between a magazine of ammo, and a clip? I do... now. Man do I know that now!)

I would also like to thank my story idea consultant - My Nephew Nicholas.

Big thanks to the guys at Utmost Studios for helping me with the cover, and promotion of this book.

Thanks to my good friend Becky for holding no ill will for killing off her character in the first chapter. Hey, you did say you wanted to be in the book!

Finally, I have to send a shout out to my Facebook Focus Group, you guys really helped me get this thing reader ready.

This novel was written during NaNoWriMo
(National Write a Novel Month)

1

The night was bitter cold, I remember that vividly. It was the kind of cold that climbs inside you and hangs there in a fog. Its icy grip reaches from your lungs up to your throat, cutting you from bones to teeth, and every breath is crisp, vivid pain.

I remember the cold, but more than that I remember the warmth. The warmth of my hands as I lifted them to my face hoping that the blood running from them was a nightmare. It was not. The weight of that reality forced me to my knees next to the beautiful horror that was lying so peacefully on the pavement.

The knife I held fell from my grip, clattering to the ground. The knife I had plunged into the most precious gift I ever received. The only person who could make me think that maybe God does exist, and love really is all we need. I'm still not sure about God, but I knew then there must be a Heaven, because I had entered Hell. I murdered my wife.

No, that wasn't true. I told myself over and over again it wasn't true. She asked me to, she begged me. I was holding the knife, but she drove it in herself. It was the next part that was mine, and this was no longer my wife.

That wasn't my wife laying on the ground next to me, her life draining from her chest. Those were not her beautiful green eyes that now stared at me soulless and empty. Her fiery red hair now darkened and matted with blood. Those were not her full red lips twitching, mouthing breathless words. This was not her, just what was left. My hand fumbled blindly for my knife as I shakily began to force my limbs into obedience.

As I gripped the weapon once again, I saw that the blood had stopped pouring from her chest, and the wound had begun to close. My wife was healing. Not my wife I told myself again. I was now on one knee, forcing myself closer to it. It was just a husk, a damned monster that only looked like her.

The eyes began to flutter back to life, but remained soulless and dim, as I reached for her blood soaked hair. My grip tightened on the hair above her scalp, and her lips formed a snarl as she uttered a guttural inhuman sound. It uttered an inhuman sound. "Isaaaac." It growled as my knife reached her throat. Its throat.

"Not my wife... you are not my wife." I sobbed as I drew the knife across the things throat. I leaned close and whispered in her ear "I am so sorry, and I love you so much... we'll be together again somehow. We have to be." After I had done my part I collapsed to the ground and surrendered to the empty blackness that my life had now become.

2

You know some of this story already – The whole world got sick, I'm sure you noticed. I say the whole world, but of course, that wasn't exactly the case. When major cities around the world became infected it seemed so surreal. When Los Angeles and the surrounding areas were put under quarantine it was like a bad dream I couldn't wake up from. When people I knew were healthy one day and dead the next it became all too real.

The worst of it was the lack of answers. Every day watching the news and seeing the parade of experts who seemed to know just as little as the rest of us about the strange disease. They debated its origins, the pattern of infection, there were even different opinions on how it was spread. And all the while we sat, cut off from the world, never knowing if we would live or not.

I say we sat, but that wasn't true of my wife. I swear, sometimes I feel like she had the strongest sense of purpose when things were at their worst. She was always a dreamer, sometimes even flighty, but when the sickness hit she held our neighborhood together nearly singlehandedly.

She insisted on spending so much time helping others that had gotten sick, I knew it was inevitable that she would as well. She was my world, and when she first showed symptoms I could feel that world collapsing around me. I think she comforted me more than I did her, but as the days went by I wondered how long her unwavering optimism could last. Then we saw the man on the T.V.

You saw too of course, but I don't know if you saw him the way we did. He stood at a press conference in a neatly pressed suit as dark blue as the deep sea, with strong features and a fierce smile. As he talked about his private corporation, and their stem cell research that provided a stunningly simple answer to the disease, he looked like hope itself. The answer was simple, and yet complex, he said. Stop trying to identify and find a cure for this one particular disease, and find a way to battle disease itself.

Their solution was to give the body the ability to revert and reformat cells to battle the sickness, using a process they developed as an alternative to traditional stem cell research. Essentially they gave the body extra resources to accomplish the task it was designed for – to maintain and repair itself.

I don't know what you thought when you first saw the reports, maybe you found it unbelievable, but I was grasping at straws at the time, and was becoming less skeptical in my desperation. When they first sent people in to administer the treatment I took Rebecca to one of the treatment centers with a strange mix of reluctance to believe in a miracle, and a hope that I was wrong. When the treatment appeared to work, I can't explain how it felt. We were all so relieved that the worst was over. How stupid we all were.

Communications both in and out of the quarantined areas have been suspended, supposedly to avoid mass panic, but before we lost the news feeds we were told that the virus had responded to the breakthrough treatment in a truly horrifying way and had become something else altogether.

We were assured that the cure could still battle the new outbreak, it just had to be improved.

It was torture watching the news, hoping for word that a cure had been found, but when we lost all contact to the outside world, T.V, internet, even phone calls, that was when we first started to feel alone. We heard rumors that people were going mad, turning into monsters. Things began to get out of control, and we did our best to stick together, and protect each other.

Teams of scientists and medical personnel were assembled by the corporation to cross into the quarantined areas around the world to study the new disease and administer new treatments. The original treatment centers were naturally located in hospitals, but they became unsecure against this new threat. The new centers were located mostly at military bases, and a small army of security was brought with them to secure the facilities against the infected who had turned.

They sacrificed themselves to help us at ground zero, but no one told us that many of our supposed saviors were the very ones who had damned us from the beginning.

3

Zombies – that's what we called them at first, but that's not what they are. I would give anything for a simple zombie apocalypse. But this is not the movies, this is something far worse. Most of us that are left have taken to calling them the Haunted.

We took the name from the first, most basic, symptom. It started as simply as nightmares. Not exactly groundbreaking I know, but they are so much more than just bad dreams. Past traumas, scenes from your life, everything you regret and fear haunts you until you just stop sleeping. Nightmares become hallucinations, as you are visited by those you've loved and lost, those you've failed. We refer to this stage as The Call because it is during this stage that the madness calls out to you, asking you to embrace it.

My own visitations usually involve my wife. Sometimes she is wearing the clothes she wore that night, sometimes the green floral sundress I loved to see her in, and sometimes she is in her wedding dress. Sometimes she wants to tell me she loves me, other times she is scared and wanting me to just hold her, but sometimes her purpose is darker. I know this is just the madness disguising itself as her, tempting me to come closer, to embrace it. That's how it works.

The next stage in the process was seen as miraculous at first. Eventually the cure went beyond simply defeating disease. It started slowly; cuts and bruises went away faster than they should, but soon it became so much more. Tissue, even organs, regenerated. Bones healed, limbs regrew, and at an astonishing rate. The treatment was designed to fight sickness, but instead healed everything. This manmade immortality came at a very steep price however.

From sickness to violence, nothing kills you, but you feel every ounce of pain. There are those, of who my wife was one, who believe the soul is eternal. However you may feel on that subject let me assure you that this body isn't supposed to be. It does something to them, feeling pain but never seeing scars. It just… breaks them somehow.

Some people think that the mind is unable to comprehend immortality and suffers a break with reality. Others say it must be some kind of physical change that happens to the brain, and alters the mind. Either way, they usually begin inflicting harm to themselves, often by cutting. The more they try to harm themselves, the more they see the futility of it, and the deeper they sink into the break until reality is gone. What happens next is also a topic of some debate.

There is no way to know why they become violent because at this stage speech, and rational thought, is lost. Whatever the reason is, they become increasingly violent, although bloodthirsty is probably a better word for it. Which is unfortunate, because the treatment started doing more than just reformatting cells to repair bones, and tissue. The body could add muscle when the situation called for it, and people became stronger, faster, not exactly superhuman, but not as far from it as we would have liked.

If you are reading this, and you have not experienced this firsthand you probably think I am exaggerating or lying about what has happened here, and I don't blame you. I truly wish I was. Maybe it's useless, because words fail me as I try to describe the horror of it all.

I can't make you feel what it is like to watch the most caring, and beautiful person you have ever met slowly lose her sanity. To have that person beg you to bury a knife in her chest so her soul won't be trapped in the body of a murderer. To promise your wife that you will remove her head to keep her from reviving and hurting anyone. I can't explain that, and you can't understand that. What I can tell you is whatever they told you happened here is a lie.

I doubt this will ever make it out of the quarantine zone, and even if it does it may be too late already, but I'm close to turning myself and don't exactly have anything else to do, so I feel the need to speak for the dead who will likely never have their story told.

4

My name is Isaac. I was forced to kill my own wife to keep her from becoming a monster, and I have spent all my time from then until now determined to make those responsible pay for their actions. Those are all the facts about me that matter.

A friend once told me that everything we once were died when the Haunted took over. What we did, who we were, who we knew, was all irrelevant now. All that mattered was who you could be, what you would do, and who you could help.

Because of his words I won't waste time telling any of my personal history, or the histories of the characters in my little narrative. Instead you will hear only of our history from the time of the Haunted on. Everything else is just the distant dreams of a different time.

My wife's name was Rebecca. I could fill volumes trying to tell you about her, but it is still too painful. I'll only say that she was the most caring person I have ever known. She saw the world in a light I have never been able to. She had a concrete faith in God that I could never shake no matter how much I doubted, or even ridiculed it. She had an inner joy I could not understand, and so at times I resented it, but now I find it's one of the things I miss most about her.

For a time I remained angry at God for allowing someone so devoted to Him to suffer like that. Now I feel my anger is a dishonor to the faith she clung to so tightly. This was the work of man not God. I only hope that her faith was justified, and that death for her is not a prison, but freedom itself. Many nights since then I have struggled with the fact that I have trouble seeing death in this light.

Death for me is the unknown, and when I try to comprehend it, to imagine the small details of what life after it would entail, I just can't. I so often commented on the absurdity of her beliefs. I thought they were nothing more than a crutch for the weak. Now in the presence of death or something even worse, I can't help but feel like the weak one.

In the early days we had stayed in Los Angeles, and made frequent trips to the treatment center at Los Angeles Air Force Base. My wife began showing symptoms well before I did, and I became frantic in my insistence that she get daily treatment. It was never easy, as the centers were often overrun with people seeking treatment, but I kept her visits as frequent as possible.

In the early stages the amounts of Haunted were a small percentage of the population. They were enough to terrify, but the military stepped in to secure the city, and they were controlled. The numbers began to increase daily, and when the military began to hear to the Call we fled in a mass exodus. With the higher populations cities had become nothing but concrete killing fields.

Those early days were filled with panic and confusion, and sadly the days since have not improved much. We were so ill equipped to handle what was happening that I am still amazed that any of us made it out alive.

We learned much about the monsters called Haunted during that time. When someone hears the Call of the Haunted they will sometimes retain those things that have become most natural to them, and return to the area most familiar to their subconscious. Those, like Rebecca and I, who frequented the treatment centers daily, would still make the trip as Haunted. As a result the centers were soon under daily attack.

The security charged with protecting the medical teams locked the facilities down. The centers became fortresses, and focused solely on research rather than treatment. Visitors were no longer allowed, and were often shot on sight.

Those in the military who turned would often retain the abilities that had become second nature to them. Fighting skills, strategies; some would even continue to use weapons. We were truly on our own.

At the time we were solely fixated on escaping the deathtrap that Los Angeles had become, and we neglected to prepare ourselves very well. We found ourselves with limited weapons and provisions, with no mode of transportation except our feet. Parties soon developed as ill prepared survivors banded together to stand a better chance against the monsters. This too was folly.

The main difference between this epidemic and the nonsense of Hollywood is that we had no idea how this disease was spread. It didn't seem to be viral, or spread by contact. There were no bites to serve as warning, and considering the situation nightmares were not seen as unusual at first, let alone a symptom.

We had no way of telling who would turn next, and this began to sow distrust and suspicion among the groups. Now I know the sickening truth that we were all infected from the beginning, and some just take longer to turn than others. To this day I am not sure why. What I do know is that whoever you are, and however you have come to be in possession of this account, you are very likely infected as well. They have lied to you. There is no disease. The cure is the disease.

5

My wife died while we were still attempting our escape from the city, and in my state of grief I made little progress. It was only through the charity of a few individuals who took pity on me, and shared from their own limited supplies, that I survived at all. After a couple of weeks I did begin to gain some control over my faculties, and began to again make my way out of the city. It may seem odd, or even absurd, that it would take weeks to flee a city on foot, but you would have to see it to truly understand the chaos that took hold.

We were fleeing in droves, and the crowds only served to draw the attention of the Haunted. From the slaughters of the crowds we learned one of the most frightening truths about the supposed disease. Those who were slaughtered violently by the Haunted soon began to heal and return as Haunted themselves. Death, especially a violent one, only triggers the Call in a more rapid manner. This made their number begin to grow exponentially, and soon the streets were overrun.

The next truth we learned was possibly the most terrifying yet. A very small fraction of the Haunted maintained some semblance of higher brain function. They could talk, although it was most often nonsensical; perhaps past conversations replaying over and over again in their broken mind.

A very small fraction of those higher functioning Haunted could do more than just rehash the past. A very small portion would actually try to reason with us. They would tell us that our eyes were closed to the truth, and that they could show us the truth behind this life, through death. I have only seen three "Talkers" in my time, and I never wish to see another. They are the most terrifying abomination that has been unleashed upon us.

We soon learned not to move in crowds, and began to make our way more cautiously through side streets and abandoned buildings, and rarely stayed long on the open streets. This made for extremely slow going, and should serve to explain the length of time it took just to escape from the city.

Two things began to occur in this now even more dire circumstance. The first was that those who survived the massacres began to think less about escape, and more about survival over a long duration of time. Supplies were gathered, weapons were procured, and we began to fight back.

This brought about the second occurrence however, and it led to even more chaos. Gangs began to take control of vital areas. Food and weapons had become priceless commodities, and those who controlled them became the tycoons of our twisted new survivalist economy.

The gangs would fortify the local super all purpose convenience center, or sporting goods/gun emporium, or in some cases whole malls. They would then charge outrageous fees for their goods, and they did not deal in cash. If you wanted guns and ammo you paid in foodstuffs. If you needed food you paid in guns and ammo, and if you needed both you were just plain out of luck. This made gathering supplies and weapons difficult for me, and I had to get pretty creative to avoid the gang controlled areas of the city.

Los Angeles' downtown was a dead zone, and very few were brave enough to venture to the site of the worst massacres, and therefore the largest amount of Haunted. The inner city area was mostly controlled by the same gangs that had always controlled it, but the farther out from the city you went the more diverse the gangs became.

Several groups controlled the suburbs made up of mostly ex military, and survivalist types that were just as ruthless as the inner city gangs. Some were more diverse groupings of regular people, but trust was not a common thing in those uncertain times, and so they were as distrusting to outsiders as the gangs and less likely to do business. The highways outside the city were regulated by biker gangs who provided secure roads to travel, but required most of your supplies in exchange for using them.

This was the uneasy state of my world. It had me scouring the city for unoccupied hardware stores to make weapons, and subsisting on whatever scraps of left behind food I could find in unoccupied houses.

Three and a half weeks after my wife's passing I had collected a sufficient amount of food, and had a small arsenal of homemade weapons. I decided it was time to make my escape from the city. I had made it as far as Burbank and had managed to avoid any gangs, or even groups up to this point. The neighborhood I was in had formerly been home to many LAPD officers who wanted to maintain close proximity to their job, but keep some distance between their families and the people they interacted with in the course of their work.

When the military started going down most of the law enforcement went with them, but some had managed to make it back to their families, and had joined together to fortify the neighborhood and help those fleeing. Although most were still committed to serving and protecting, and were a much more welcome site than the gangs, they did not take kindly to people looting houses in their neighborhood.

Since that was exactly what I was doing, I was moving very cautiously through the area. After I had collected my last few resources I began to make my way to the nearest freeway exit, intending to sneak onto interstate 5 and follow it out to the less populated cities to the North. It was here, outside a little apartment complex, that I first met Doc.

He looked to be in his fifties with crew cut hair, and a rather impressive red beard with streaks of white. He stood roughly six feet tall, and was wearing a blue dress shirt and black slacks. I remember because it was a little more formal attire than I was used to seeing. He wasn't fat, but I wouldn't call him thin either, more like thick. Not imposing, but not unimpressive.

He approached the gate of the complex, and pressed the buzzer for one of the apartments. I was down the street a little ways hiding behind a vehicle, so I could not see which number he pressed, but I could see even from where I was that he was nervous. That was pretty understandable considering the circumstance. Behind him was a man holding a shotgun to his back, and he looked very imposing.

6

The man with the shotgun was at least six two, and outweighed his hostage by no less than sixty pounds. He was not dressed nearly as fancy as the man he held at gun point. Instead he wore boots, jeans, urban camouflage vest, and an unpleasant scowl that screamed military surplus.

The captive got no reply from his buzzer press, turned and shrugged at his captor who urged him to try again by pressing the shotgun barrel into his back. After a few more buzzes and about five minutes he must have got a reply, although I could not hear it, because military surplus pushed him out of the way and pressed the intercom with some force as he bellowed his reply.

I had no problem making his words out from my hiding spot behind a black SUV. "Well now I got something you will want to trade for, so get down here! Trust me; you're going to want to see this for yourself."

The situation was getting interesting at this point, and I could not resist the urge to sneak a little closer. There was a beat up red truck about twenty feet ahead, and maybe thirty feet from the action, and I made my way to it unseen. After a few more minutes the gate opened, and a group of five men with automatic weapons filed out, followed by a sixth that I assumed to be the leader.

They were bikers, and every one cut just as imposing a figure as surplus did. Surplus was the first to speak. "I want to renegotiate the terms of my transportation fee" he said with a smirk. He obviously liked trying to sound fancy, but big words just sounded less intelligent when placed in his mouth.

Unfortunately this confirmed what I had feared; the bikers had this entrance blocked, and this was a checkpoint of sorts. I needed to get away from here, and see if I could find a blind spot to bypass this checkpoint, but I just couldn't pull myself away from the proceedings. The leader stepped forward past his entourage.

He was as large as any of them with a beard that was nothing short of magnificent at nearly three feet long. I don't know how the bikers chose their leaders, but I like to think beard length was a significant factor. As he made his reply he let out a thick booming laugh.

"Well, Buck it seems the bigger your words get the dumber you sound. When I told you we needed supplies in fair exchange for your use of our road system that is not exactly what I had in mind. I don't know how things are done in whatever hick infested backwater you were raised in, but here we don't consider people foodstuffs." The bikers all let out laughs nearly as booming as their leader's. I couldn't help thinking that even Buck's name sounded like it had been purchased at a military surplus.

Buck was unfazed by the insults, and continued on with his smirk still in place. "I think you might change yer mind when you get to know my guest a little more. This is you biker's lucky day, this right here is some kinda doc straight from the treatment center here to save all of us from the big bad virus."

That is when I realized that the situation had just become far more complicated, and dire. After a pause to let his bombshell sink in Buck continued. "That's right, you remember the guys who come riding in here promising that they could fix us, and just ended up making everything worse? They told us they could help, and then when it all went to crap they hid behind their thugs and shot anybody who came looking for answers. Some help right? Your girl was one them that was shot like that weren't she Esau?"

Esau, I had heard his name before. He was not just the leader of this checkpoint but of the entire gang, at least of the gang that held interstate 5. Some of the other roads were held by rival gangs but all the roads on this side of town were held by Esau's group, and I had somehow found the one checkpoint with him in it.

I edged to the front of the truck I was using as cover to hear Esau's reply.

His countenance had grown darker as he edged closer to Buck. His voice was lower, and his tone was deadly serious. "Tread softly Buck."

It was only three words but the effect was instantaneous, Buck threw his hands up in surrender. When he did I saw Doc twitch ever so slightly as he thought for a split second about going Buck's gun, but changed his mind, probably on account of the other five men with guns. One hick with a shotty, and five bikers with autos, and he was thinking about making a move! I was starting to like Doc at that point.

Buck's reply was hurried and apologetic. "Hey, no offense intended, alls I'm saying is I got one of the cowards responsible right here, and I think we might come to an agreement."

It was at this moment that Doc spoke up with far more rancor in his voice than I would advise anyone being held at gunpoint to use. "First of all, I am a Physician's Assistant not a Doctor, and I helped administer treatments and handle checkups. I didn't design it. Also, if I was hiding in the treatment center then I wouldn't be in this situation, now would I? Secondly, I haven't murdered anyone. That is the kind of behavior that forced me to leave the center. There are only two things I have to be ashamed of, the actions of my colleagues, and the fact that I was actually captured by an idiot like you." That was the moment when I decided that I definitely liked Doc.

Esau must have been taking a liking to him too; he let loose an uproarious laugh at Doc's impertinence. Buck was becoming exasperated as his grand scheme was falling apart. He drove the butt of his shotgun into Doc's stomach to silence him, and spoke rapidly at Esau. "It is a good deal Esau, I give you him to make an example of, and you let me leave." Buck was getting desperate.

"You just heard him Buck, he says he wasn't involved, and I believe him; besides, killing Docs ain't going to bring anybody back. I never let my emotions get the best of my business sense. Take your doc and get outta here; I'm tired of looking at your stupid face."

"So what if he weren't there? He's still one of them. Those self righteous know it alls hiding in their fort, he is one of *them*. That has to count for something."

Esau had started to turn away as Buck rambled on, but at this last statement he paused. "You know Buck that may be the first smart thing I have ever heard you say." Buck smiled at this; even though his confused look made it obvious he had no idea why it was so smart. Esau continued, talking more to himself than to Buck. "I have no use for him, but maybe his friends do. He is, after all, one of them."

At this point one of his men addressed him in a hushed tone that I barely made out. "You think they'll pay for him? I mean they did let him leave and go out on his own, what if they don't want him?"

"Way I see it we either get to trade him for some top rate supplies from the docs and their personal army, or we kill him in front of them and show them what we think of their kind. Both ways we don't really lose anything except Buck's company, and I don't consider that much of a loss."

It was not looking good for Doc at that point. I didn't think his colleagues would value his life higher than their supplies from what I had seen of their character, and the look on his face told me he felt the same way. I knew the safest thing would be to start my retreat while I still could, and distance myself from the situation, but something in me just couldn't leave him.

I began wondering what my wife would say, something biblical no doubt, probably about being a Good Samaritan, or doing unto others, or some other cliché that was likely to get me killed. I took a deep breath, and closed my eyes to think it through. I knew I had to get Doc out of there, but I didn't have the faintest clue as to how I was going to do it.

It was at this point that Buck made the mistake of thinking he had the upper hand. He decided to get greedy. "Hold on Esau, you just said this guy could be worth something, I think I should get more than just free passage."

Esau turned back to fully face Buck, and he looked like he was losing patience. Buck was pushing his luck, and I was racking my brain for a plan before this got ugly. "Just what do you have in mind Buck?" The words were pushed through his teeth as he was barely able to restrain himself.

Buck was an idiot, but even he could tell at this point that he was playing with fire, and he adopted his apologetic tone again. "Well, I mean not much, I don't want much, but my truck over there is running low on gas, and I only got those two reserve tanks in the back." Buck pointed almost directly at me as he said this, and I thought for a split second that they had seen me as I ducked back behind the front passenger tire.

After a few moments without any shouts or gunshots I decided that I had not been spotted, and poked my head over the bed of the truck slightly to see what was happening. That was when I saw the contents of Buck's truck. The two reserve tanks standing up were presumably the tanks he had just mentioned, and the three tanks lying on their sides haphazardly were obviously his empties. There were also some more shotguns, a hunting rifle, toolbox, and a few oily rags.

A plan had started to formulate in my head, but it still was going to take a tremendous stroke of luck. I lowered myself back behind the tire, as Buck and Esau were coming to an agreement that seemed fair to both parties. My time was running out. I slowly raised my eyes to the passenger window to look in the truck. "There is no way" I told myself "Not even he is that dumb." I looked into the cab, and had to refrain from laughing. There, hanging from the ignition, was Buck's key chain.

7

As the biker and the hick stood working out the fine details of the agreement I began hurriedly working on my plan. There was a group of motorcycles roughly thirty feet away, parked haphazardly over the curb, downhill from my position behind Buck's truck. The decline was fairly steep, and the bikes were positioned in a way that worked well for my plan.

I made my way to the bikes, using some of the abandoned vehicles that littered the street as cover, just as one of the bikers emerged from the gate carrying two reserve gas tanks that were apparently all the extra provisions Buck was able to negotiate for. The deal was clearly at the conclusion, and I had precious little time before Buck began walking back to his vehicle.

I am not a biker myself by any means, but I knew enough to find the fuel lines on the bikes, and begin cutting them pretty furiously with my knife. As a side note let me just say that during a zombie apocalypse, or anything close, you should always keep some reliable lighters and a nice sharp knife on hand, because you just never know when you'll need them.

At the time I was pretty panicked, and mostly just praying that my ridiculous stunt would work. I was crouched among the bikes even closer to the negotiations than I had been at Buck's truck, and with far less cover. All it would take was a glance in my direction to make it all fall apart, but my luck held and I remained unseen.

Buck's bounty was loaded into his truck while I was working on the bikes; luckily he was still trying to squeeze a few more supplies out of Esau, giving me the extra time I needed. I made sure to get a nice pool of gasoline collecting in the water runoff that ran in front of the curb. The biker loading up Buck's truck finished and returned to his boss's side, allowing me to return to my spot behind the truck.

By the time I emptied one of Buck's gas cans into the same overflow trench that ran in front of the bikes, Esau had convinced Buck that he had gotten all the supplies he was going to get. When the gasoline made its way down the run off, and connected to the pool underneath the bikes, Doc was handed over to Esau. As I lit the trail of fuel and watched it burn all the way to the group of bikes, the small group had turned from their discussion just in time to see the show.

It had the desired effect on Esau and his men, as they all moved their attention to the flames. It was no movie explosion to be sure, but the way those bikers reacted to the site of the fire dancing across their bikes was priceless. It was also all the opening I needed.

I threw my bag of supplies in the bed of my brand new beat up old truck, got in, and turned the key. I have no idea what I would have done had that old truck not turned over, but luckily it did. I threw it into drive and put the gas pedal to the floor. When he heard the tires peeling out Buck looked over and spotted me, but by the time he processed the information, and began to raise his shotgun, I was heading his way fast.

The truck cut his legs out from under him, and sent him hurtling into the windshield. He left a spider webbed collection of cracks on it that made it near impossible to see through. I didn't have enough distance to build up the speed necessary to actually kill him, but it beat him up enough that he wouldn't be impeding our escape.

Doc was looking pretty shocked at this point and just stood there frozen, so I had to give him some encouragement. "Kinda in a hurry jump in please!" I shouted sharply, and to his credit Doc got himself moving again pretty fast, and hopped up in the bed of the truck with more agility than I thought he would have in him.

Esau's gang was too preoccupied with my distraction to react in time to stop my rescue attempt. I maneuvered the truck through the group of stunned bikers with my head hanging out the window since the windshield was too smashed up to see through thanks to Buck. There were bikers falling to the concrete left and right as they jumped out of my way, and by the time they started shooting at us we were barreling down towards the road block.

When I could see the block about a half mile down the road I stopped and jumped out quickly with the engine still running. Doc started to say something to me but I cut him off. "Sorry Doc, but we don't really have the time; after we complete our escape I promise we'll make time for proper introductions. Right now I need you to grab my bag and as many of Buck's guns as you can carry, and most importantly I need you to shut up." He paused for a moment, and then set his jaw and we both worked in silence. He came around the truck with my bag and Buck's guns just as I was finishing my latest creation, and could not resist asking me what I was doing.

"If you look up the road you will see a road block run by the same biker gang that I just snatched you from. They are not likely to let us pass, so this here is my road block buster." I patted the gas tank bomb that I had sitting in the front seat. I had rigged the seat belt through the steering wheel to keep it straight and, after lighting the makeshift rag fuse; I wedged the tank onto the gas pedal and put the truck into drive.

"So what do we do now?" Doc asked still not sure of what was going on.

"Now we run, just follow my lead."

I gave the truck time to build a lead before taking off at a full sprint for the road block. They positioned their block just in front of the on ramp to the not - so - freeway. Luckily for us the city was adding another lane to this particular road back when traffic and the commute to work were the kinds of things we cared about. The construction materials and heavy equipment strewn about would provide adequate cover, at least until we reached the roadblock itself.

The truck missile stayed on course and worked even better than I could have hoped. The gas tank bomb exploded right before the truck hit its mark and flew into the line of SUVs that the bikers were using to block the road. The bikers that had been standing guard between the SUVs were sent scrambling as broken glass, scrap metal, Buck's pickup truck, and the smell of gasoline filled the air. The result was utter chaos, and the only shot we had at making it through.

We had made our way quickly, but cautiously through the construction at this point. I knew our window of confusion would be very small, but I thought it might just be enough. The pickup had only drifted off its course slightly, hitting two of the SUVs on the far left before launching into the air. This brought all of the guards to that side of the blockade, moving slowly with guns drawn and fixed on the mangled pickup.

My luck that day continued to hold as we sprinted for the unoccupied right side, because the pickup had apparently had its tank punctured in the collision, and provided one last diversion in the form of an explosion. The bewildered guards hit the dirt again, and by the time they recovered we were past the roadblock, up the on ramp, and into the cover of the abandoned vehicles that littered the freeway. Unfortunately we weren't out of the metaphorical woods yet. We were now on foot, and I was sure Esau and his goons would be coming for us.

We managed to dodge their scouts for a while as we made our way down the road, but then they brought a more systematic and organized approach. They had men from every checkpoint along the road form groups and search their sections car by car. Five miles up the road they finally had us hemmed in.

We were holed up behind some little tin can of a sports car. There was too big a gap between it and the next vehicle to make it without being seen. This stretch of road had all been elevated, so we had no way off the road. There was a group approaching from about a quarter mile on either side of us.

My luck had apparently run out. They had caught us in one of the least crowded sections we had come across. Too much open area, too little cover, and far too many men with guns. The only bright side was that along the way to our being cornered like rats, Doc and I had a chance to make formal introductions.

Apparently his name was actually Donald or Don if I preferred, and he of course informed me again that he wasn't actually a M.D, but a Physician's Assistant. When I asked him what the difference was, he told me three years of school and about thirty thousand bucks a year.

I replied that as far as I was concerned he had earned the promotion by getting caught in this mess, and Doc just had a better ring to it. I have referred to him as Doc ever since.

He had been in medicine for over thirty years before volunteering to aid the scientists and doctors of the corporation in distributing their cure. The corporation had designed it, but they were lacking the manpower needed to distribute it, and so the Government put out a call for volunteers in the medical field to assist.

Doc had been administering doses and performing follow ups since the first virus. He documented each patient's progress while the geniuses kept producing their miracle treatment. When the Haunted first began to show up he refused to be evacuated and stayed on to help where he could. He felt they owed it to us.

Apparently he was leery of the treatment from the beginning. He asked me if I was familiar with the science of the cure, but after I told him yes, he explained it to me anyway. He felt there was a flaw in reformatting cells to fight a virus, since viruses often mutate to combat the cure.

"Flu for example, every year we have to develop a new vaccine to combat the flu. That vaccine is based on whatever strain of flu virus is more prevalent that year. Basically we have to guess because the virus mutates year to year. When our bodies defeat a disease it simply mutates itself into a form our bodies haven't seen yet, often times something much worse."

Of course there was much more technical jargon in what Doc said, there always was, but I don't think I could remember it even if I tried. What he said next stood out in my memory however. Doc had recently begun to doubt his own theory, and feared that the truth was even was than he feared.

I wanted him to go on, but by that time the net was closing in, and we had strategy to discuss. "Okay Doc, looks like we have some decisions to make." He nodded his head slightly, but said nothing. "We can make our stand here, but we are outgunned, surrounded, and have inadequate cover. The smart money would not be on us making it out alive. Unfortunately, the odds of surviving another run in with Esau aren't exactly great either, and I'm afraid I'm all out of tricks."

Doc took a deep breath in through his nose, and let it out his mouth slowly. He paused for a moment and then set his jaw and nodded his head slightly, apparently coming to a decision in his mind. "Not many people would go to these lengths for a stranger. Thanks Isaac, but this is my fight. I'll draw their fire while you make a run for it." He grabbed one of Buck's shotguns that I had stuffed in my trusty blue canvas bag, and looked positively resolute.

I had to stifle a laugh at the sight of Doc preparing for his last stand. I called him Doc Holliday for at least a week afterwards. "That's a very noble gesture Doc. My only question would be run to where? There aren't many good hiding spots between us and them. No, sorry Doc but I'm as stuck as you are. Besides, you stuck your neck out and left safety to come help guys like me, so I stuck my neck out for you. For what it is worth I don't regret trying to help you at all. So what's our play? Do we take our chances with Esau, or go all Butch and Sundance on these guys?"

Doc smiled at the movie reference as he replied. "Well, I'm not looking forward to seeing him again, but I don't see any options I like better."

"It's settled then. Let's go talk to the boss."

8

They held us at the checkpoint while Esau made his way to us with his five bodyguards in tow. The bikes they rolled up on looked less barbecued than I remembered, so I assumed they had commandeered some new ones from lower ranking members of the gang. Esau looked even less enthused to see us than I had anticipated, and demonstrated this by stomping his way over to us and delivering some heavy handed punches to our midsections.

"Howdy boys, it's good to see you again." He let another punch loose in my gut to prove it. When Doc protested Esau connected on a left hook to Doc's chin that made him crumple to the ground, and then turned back to me. "We had to search pretty hard for you two." His jaw was tight, and the words were almost hissed through clenched teeth. He looked like he had been chewing glass. I decided to give him more to chew on.

"That really is an odd coincidence, because we've actually been looking all over for you too. In fact I was just telling Doc..."

"Shut up!" Esau bellowed as he brought a vicious right handed uppercut that sent me flying. After I caught my breath and picked myself up off the ground I decided to stay silent and let him talk. "You set our bikes on fire!" He was practically spitting at this point, and his tone was venomous as he continued. "That has consequences around here son. You can't just go setting fire to a man's property without paying for it, and I loved that bike so it's going to get pricey."

He went for another body blow, but I was getting tired of the monotony. As the telegraphed punch flew towards my ribs I turned my body slightly and stepped into it. The blow glanced awkwardly off as Esau's momentum brought him right into the left elbow I was bringing his jaw. The blow snapped his head back, and I quickly grabbed his shoulder with my left hand and used the leverage, and my momentum, to launch myself up and bring an elbow down onto his face. The point of my elbow smashed into his nose, and as I landed blood began pouring down his face and into his beard.

I didn't have much time to celebrate my small victory before one of his goons brought the butt of his gun into the side of my head. I went down hard, and a boot to my back told me they wanted me to stay there. Esau labored back up to his feet, and unleashed several savage kicks to my ribs. I struggled to regain my breath, and began coughing violently and spitting up blood. I hoped it was from biting my cheek or tongue when I got hit, and not from internal bleeding. The kicks subsided and I managed to get to my hands and knees. Having regained my composure somewhat, I was for the first time aware of the heat of the asphalt.

The sun was burning high in the sky, making the oil in the roads glisten. The temperature was at least high nineties, and I had just finished running several miles attempting to evade Esau and his men. I was beaten up, exhausted, and very hot; so when I tell you that what I saw when I looked up made me go cold all over, you know I'm serious. My face must have shown it too, because Esau and his men immediately followed my gaze. Behind them walking casually past the checkpoint was one of the Haunted.

Though the Haunted were terrifying both in strength and speed, not to mention healing and pure ruthless aggression, it was still unusual for just one of them to make it through one of the biker's checkpoints that easily. They had been so focused on Doc and I that they let their guard down, and left only a couple men on watch. To make matters worse this Haunted was one of the military personnel brought in to deal with the Haunted, which of course meant that he probably retained at least some of his training. This was confirmed by the Ka-bar knife in his right hand.

Given that their regenerative abilities keep their bodies in top condition, despite the fact they never sleep or eat, you would think it would be harder to identify them. It is hard to put into words, but there is a soullessness to their features you can spot even from a distance. The way they move is just different somehow. I can't explain it, but even though they look like us, there is a quality to them that is easily recognizable as inhuman.

Esau and his men brought their guns up in a panic, and the first shots were erratic to say the least. The Haunted ran for cover behind a nearby sedan at a shocking speed. The bikers had no chance to land a good shot, let alone a head shot.

That is the final thing you should know about the Haunted, and the only one that is reminiscent of the movies, the only way to kill them is to take out the head. Since the brain is the command center of the body, if it's not sending out signals, the cells won't regenerate. Removing the head of something that is stronger and faster than you, self-healing, and determined to kill you, however, is much easier said than done.

The thing waited until the men had emptied their magazines and were reloading, then in a horrific show of power ripped the passenger door off the sedan and hurled it at the gunmen. The men scattered to avoid the flying hunk of metal, and showing it was easily as fast as it was strong, the Haunted followed close behind the door and was suddenly in the midst of the men. Before they could reload their weapons it tore through them. The five bikers that made up Esau's personal guard were cut to ribbons with the sweeping motions of its blade.

While they were falling the rest of the men had managed to reload their weapons. Shotguns and automatic weapons sprayed the air with bullets, but they were useless against the Haunted. Effortlessly it grabbed two of Esau's fallen bodyguards and threw them in the path of their fire, and soon it was among them darting to and fro, butchering them with ease.

Blood stained the asphalt as the few who remained dropped their weapons and ran for their lives from the creature. The Haunted let out an animalistic cry and raised its blood soaked hands to the sky. Its body was covered in blood and bullet holes, but none of the men had managed to hit the target that mattered. None of them shot it in the head.

It turned back towards Esau and I could see the bullet holes closing as it strolled up to us with a wicked smile playing across its face. Esau had been thrown against the guardrail in the initial attack, and had just made it back to his feet and collected his gun when the creature began walking towards him.

As he raised the gun, the thing moved quickly and he was only able to squeeze off three rounds before it reached him. Two of the shots hit it in the chest, but the third hit him in the head; unfortunately for Esau it must have missed any of the critical parts that kept the creature functioning because it kept coming. It swatted the gun away, grabbed him by the throat, and lifted the large man into the air.

Doc and I had also been thrown aside in the initial attack, and had stayed low when the bullets began to fly. This was the perfect opportunity to get away, but I found myself conflicted. Esau had just beaten us, and was very likely going to kill us, but no one deserved this.

While I was hesitating on what course to take Doc had apparently come to his decision already and charged past me towards Esau. Even in those dire straits I had to marvel at Doc charging headlong towards a monster just to save a man who was possibly going to kill him earlier. I knew I could not let Doc take that thing on alone, but I had no idea how we were going to take it out.

As I chased after Doc I saw Esau's new bike standing not twenty feet from the struggle, and made a mad dash for it. By the time I had gotten to it and got it started Doc had already done his best imitation of a linebacker and tackled the Haunted into the guard rail. It released its grip on Esau and he scampered away. The beast let out an angry cry and backhanded Doc nearly ten feet away from him.

As soon as Doc was clear, I accelerated, and at the last second put the bike into a slide sending both it and the creature crashing into the guardrail. The bike wasn't heavy enough, or going fast enough, to break through the guardrail; instead, it pinned the Haunted against it. I knew I only had an instant. The bike had likely crushed several of its bones, but they would be healing quickly. I got up from my slide and ran towards the thing.

In one fluid movement I scooped up the knife it had dropped, used the bike as a jumping board to launch myself in the air, and with two hands brought the knife over my head and then down into its face with all my force. As the Haunted stared up me with malice, my knife slid into its right eye socket. The blade sank deep, and I began furiously repeating the blow again and again while the creature let out a shriek that was a mixture of frustration, pain, and rage.

I began shoving the blade upwards through the blood and mush that was the Haunted's face, trying to pierce the brain. When I was sure the thing was finally dead I fell backwards to the ground, falling over the motorcycle, exhausted and covered in blood.

9

There was a moment when I wasn't sure Doc and I had made the right choice in coming back for Esau. The men from the next checkpoint heard the gunshots from our battle with the Haunted, and had sent a patrol our way. They came before Doc and I were able to collect ourselves, and impeded our departure. They held us at gunpoint while Esau slowly made his way over.

"You two have caused me a lot of trouble today" He turned towards me "your little fireworks display earlier attracted a lot of attention from the Haunted, and because we were so focused on capturing you two one of em was able to waltz in here and butcher some of my best men." He paced for a moment and then turned back to me and became more animated as he spoke. "I don't even know who you are, or why you're so determined to save the doc here."

I immediately stuck my hand out. "The names Isaac. Good Samaritan, apparent friend to the medical community, and all around nice guy, good to meet ya."

He replied by shoving my hand out of the way and telling me to shut up, but it was said with much less force this time, and I could tell he was holding back a smile. We were growing on ol' Esau.

"You two have seriously never met before? Cause you seem as thick as thieves."

Doc spoke up at this point. "No we haven't, and that's unfortunate because he seems to be one of the few people around here who hasn't lost their humanity along with the Haunted."

Esau shook his head and chuckled. "You got some brave words Doc, I'm starting to think you enjoy testing my patience." He turned from Doc and pointed at me. "And you! Don't think I have forgotten that you lit my bike on fire, and used my replacement bike like a battering ram."

"I've got a nice truck I just recently acquired that I'll trade you. It was in a bit of a fender bender recently, minor cosmetic damage mostly. It still runs like a dream though."

Esau tried to restrain his laugh, but failed. "Seeing that idiot's face when he saw what you did to his truck was almost worth all the other damage you caused. Almost. You two came back to help me when you didn't have to and I won't forget that, but I think you still owe me some compensation, so here is what we are going to do. You two are gonna go on some supply missions. You procure some goods for us, we give you your freedom and everybody is happy."

"I have a different deal in mind." The voice came from behind us and when I turned I had to do a double take. Earlier in the conversation I'd heard some more bikers ride up, but took no notice of who had entered the fray until now. The man who spoke, and was walking to our little group, was the spitting image of Esau. He had a group of bikers with him also, and they all circled around where Doc, Esau, and I were having our conversation.

Esau walked towards the man, stretched out his hand and smiled. "Good to see you Jacob."

The man smiled in return "You too brother."

Jacob must have seen the look on my face, because he let out a hearty laugh and said to me. "You heard right, we are twin brothers."

"Named Jacob and Esau?"

"Mother was extremely religious, and Father had a strange sense of humor. Glad you know the reference though, not everybody does these days." He turned his attention back towards his brother. "Glad you're okay. We were coming back from the city when we saw what was left of the roadblock, and the men there told us what happened."

Esau cut him off. "And let me guess, you came rushing here to tell me to let the doctor go, and preach at me about the evils of my little business venture. Problem is I'm getting real tired of your sermons."

Jacob held up his hands in surrender "Okay, okay, I didn't come to rehash old arguments; I heard on the radio that gunshots were heard from this way. I don't have all the details but from what I can tell these men saved you when they could have made an escape. You owe these men your life, and you're trying to bargain with them?"

Esau set his jaw hard, and the veins in his head were starting to become visible. "I recognize they stayed when they could have run, but the trouble was still mostly their doing anyway. Why reward them for cleaning up their own mess?"

"Because they saved my brother's life, that's why. I love you bro, but you need to learn when to just say thank you. I tell you what, you like making deals, so let's make a deal."

"Go on." Esau said, clearly interested.

"I'll pay what they owe, and in return they will escort my men and me out of the city."

Esau laughed. "Escort you? What, you mean like bodyguards?" He let out another loud laugh. "Sorriest looking security team I've ever seen."

"I don't know, they sure did a number on you and your men." That cut the laughter short

"Fine, you want to add some more charity cases to your little salvation army there, go ahead, but don't think I won't make you pay."

"You always do. Well assuming that these two have no problem lending me their talents then we will be on our merry way."

10

Jacob was a constant surprise, and pretty much the polar opposite of his twin brother. He had never approved of Esau's road blocks, but he knew that his brother was not likely to see reason, and forcing him to stop would simply mean another gang would step in. Jacob decided instead to help those fleeing the city by negotiating with Esau.

Every so often Jacob would lead a party into the city to gather as many supplies as possible. They would also collect as many survivors as they could, and would pay their toll out of the supplies they collected. Those survivors once out of the city would help Jacob distribute the rest of the goods at different locations in the smaller surrounding cities. The locations tended to be churches, or groups of Christians holed up in whatever shelter they could find to act as a church. This explained Esau's nicknaming them the "Salvation Army." It also helped to explain most of the animosity between the brothers. Before the Haunting Esau's line of work was quite similar to his current occupation, and for a long time Jacob was at his side. When he got saved that changed, and the rift only grew in the decade that followed.

Jacob had about thirty men in his crew who were regulars and twenty five or so that he added to the group in L.A. Everyone that traveled in Jacob's caravan was required to pull their weight, not just in acquiring and transporting goods, but also in defense. Having fifty to sixty guns is a major benefit, but the downside is that you tend to attract attention.

Carrying such large amounts of food, weapons, and people made things difficult as well. Most of the men in Jacob's regulars were riding motorcycles for their ability to navigate the wreckage and abandoned cars with ease, but the supplies and extra travelers required larger modes of transportation. They had one large bus full of supplies and people, and smaller trucks or SUVs trailing behind carrying the rest.

Being unsure of my own beliefs I was leery of traveling with the bible thumping biker, but the only thing more impressive than his knowledge of the bible was his compassion towards people. He never pushed his faith on us, but we did have numerous discussions on the subject. He and Doc were a lot of fun to listen to once they got going, and they often bantered well into the night.

We made our way north helping Jacob deliver supplies in each new town, and gathering more supplies for the next town. The system the churches had was actually quite impressive. We stopped at each church to give them supplies, and if they had excess of anything they gave it to us for the next church and so on down the chain. It was like the desperate times helped the church to shake off the apathy, and operate the way it was supposed to.

Those whose toll he paid would help out for awhile and leave when they reached their destination, although some decided to stay on permanently. We weren't all believers, but we were all welcome, and it was difficult to stay around Jacob very long without some measure of belief rubbing off.

A few towns into this process Doc gave me the information that changed everything. We were on the road heading into Palmdale, and had stopped for the night. The temperature was a pleasant seventy degrees, and the moon was bright so we set up camp there on the road. We posted guards on each side of the road, and worked in two man teams rotating in three hour shifts.

Doc and I took the first shift, and I took the opportunity to bring up the conversation we had never finished from when we first met. It had been bugging me ever since that first day, but we had been so since we first signed on with Jacob, there hadn't really been time to discuss it. We sat on the tailgate of a red pickup, looking out on the expanse of road that wound through the gentle hills, weeds, and sand of the desert. There were no more lights anymore, nothing but a full moon that turned the desert a pale blue, and gave the road an almost purple hue.

"Doc, I've been meaning to ask you about something. Something you told me the first time we met. That the truth about this disease could be worse than anyone imagined."

"I figured you wouldn't let that go." He said with a chuckle. "I assumed we'd have to discuss this eventually, but you should know that I don't have any evidence, only my logic and suspicions, and a few cryptic statements."

"I understand."

"Well, the first thing is that I don't believe it is a disease making these monsters. I think it is purely a reaction to the treatment. The disease could in fact mutate to the cure, but it shouldn't happen this fast. I think that for reasons I don't quite understand, the mind itself is rejecting this cure, and causing a kind of break with reality."

"Man's body is not meant to be immortal, only his soul." Doc and I both turned in surprise to see that Jacob had snuck up on us. "Sorry to eavesdrop, but I couldn't sleep so I figured I'd come help you guys keep watch, but I didn't mean to butt in on your conversation."

"Not at all" Doc quickly replied "Go ahead."

Doc and I were sitting on the tailgate of a stranded pickup truck, so Jacob hopped up on the trunk of little foreign hybrid that was next to us, and tried to get comfortable. "I know this is going to sound like religious nut talk, but our mind operates on the premise that this life is finite. This is what makes notions like Heaven and Hell, and God impossible to comprehend. We can't process it with our limited understanding because we think in terms of beginning and end.

"So now we take the finite mind and body, and make it infinite. We think we have found the fountain of youth, but instead we have condemned our souls to this earthly prison. We are so afraid of death that we have forgotten that it is what makes life so priceless. Why do you two always look at me like that when I get philosophical?"

"No reason, I just didn't know they had a biker seminary." I said laughing.

"Shut up."

"Turn the other cheek brother."

"Don't make me hurt you Isaac."

"That doesn't seem very Christian"

"I'll pray for forgiveness later" He laughed. "Fine, I'll stop spouting off, and let you finish Doc."

Doc smiled. "It's fine. You could very well be right, I honestly don't know. I'm not sure how much it even matters anymore." He looked more solemn than I was used to from Doc. "I'm sorry if I sound overly dramatic." He said while managing a weak smile. "It's just that if my second conclusion is true…"

"What's your second conclusion Doc?" It was starting to unnerve me how much this conversation seemed to be rattling Doc. I wondered what information could do that to him, and what could possibly be worse than the official story. I got my answer.

"My second conclusion is that the disease that started this was designed. I'll spare you the technical jargon, but the way it has reacted, the areas it has hit, and the timeframe of the infections, plus whisperings around the research center all lead me to believe that this virus was created and released intentionally."

Needless to say these were some pretty shocking statements, and Doc must have read it in our faces because he quickly added "I know it is a lot to take in, and as I said I have no proof and no idea how to attain any. All I have are my conclusions, and I'm sorry that I'm just dumping them on you without much build up."

Jacob replied first. "I haven't known you too long Doc, but I trust your instincts. You are a smart guy, and if you have enough to draw those conclusions then that is enough for me."

It was at this point that I jumped in. "So, assuming you're right Doc, who spread the disease, a terrorist organization? I mean who would have the resources for such a widespread release?"

Doc took a deep breath, and let it out slowly while closing his eyes. I had seen this operation before; he did this whenever he was faced with a tough decision. I realized that he still hadn't fully decided if he should say the next part.

"Let me put it this way. If you had actually found a way to cure disease, all disease, and you needed to find a way to showcase it to the world, while at the same time bypassing all the red tape and tests that would delay the release of your wonder drug…"

"You can't be serious."

"Why not Jacob? Think about it, why settle for a Nobel when you could have the entire world at your feet? That corporation was being touted as saviors before everything turned ugly, and the way they have spun the truth they probably will still come out like heroes. We are not just talking money, this will earn them political power and fame galore."

"Still, you really think they would put millions of lives on the line for politics and fame?" This time it was my question.

"It wouldn't be the first time in history that has happened. First they show up with an experimental drug that is still in testing phase, yet they are able to mass produce it on a global level. When people start turning into monsters they lie about the Haunted, and blame it on the disease. And when the Haunted problem gets out of control they hide in the facilities and none of them get sick. The military brought in to take care of the Haunted turned, but the security detail assigned to protect them hasn't as far as I know. Why is that?"

"They locked themselves away, maybe they haven't been infected?" Jacob offered.

"Not likely, the amount of time that we spent around the initial disease, and even once the Haunted came into the picture, to think that not one of us got infected is pretty absurd. If they were worried about becoming infected I don't think they would have brought in the people who had been in the field, like me."

"So they never gave you guys the treatment?" Jacob questioned.

"They did, or at least that is what they said. I think they were lying to us. I don't think any of the medical personnel ever received the treatment, at least not the one everyone else got."

"So if you didn't have the cure how come none of you got the virus?" I asked

"I think they have a way to combat the virus other than the cure, which is one more reason I think they designed the virus themselves. I think they told us we were receiving the treatment, but in truth they gave us a cure only for the virus. I know this sounds farfetched, but I hope you'll indulge me a little further."

I couldn't believe it. "You mean there is more?"

"I am afraid so, and it will be the most troubling and hardest to believe, because I don't believe they are done. I think there is a hidden power behind this corporation, and think they have goals beyond just creating a virus to promote a cure."

"What kind of goals?"

"Unfortunately, I have no idea. I have been asking myself that same question, but I only have rumors to go on."

"Maybe you should start at the beginning then, and tell us what you heard."

11

The conversation spanned the rest of our shift on watch, and doesn't need to be transcribed word for word. Doc's fears started soon after they first retreated into the facilities. The medical personnel that had been doing the dirty work basically became glorified lab assistants and go-fors to the researchers and biologists working on a new cure.

The facility had access to a camera network that included traffic cams, some security feeds, and a few others that the researchers had set up themselves. Doc wasn't sure on the technical aspect of how they managed it, but they were able to have eyes on almost the whole city.

They would have several volunteers and corporation docs sit down, study, and record the habits of the Haunted, and those who heard the Call and turned. It was of course unpleasant work, so they worked in teams of two, switching often to keep from having to watch the horror too long. It also helped with the boredom for the long stretches when there was nothing on their cameras.

"Sometimes the pairing would be two volunteers, and sometimes one volunteer and one researcher. We would try to pass the time with small talk, sports, politics anything basically. I got to know one of the researchers pretty well. I can't tell you his name because I told him I never would, but he was a brilliant Geneticist. We had very similar points of view on many subjects, and we tried to pair up as often as possible over the next couple weeks. On one of these times I got going on my soap box, as I had a tendency of doing in those days, and began railing on the government." He paused briefly, shook his head and laughed softly to himself.

"He used to call me the anti government government worker. I had volunteered to be brought in by the government to help, and I had practiced medicine in the Air Force for some years, but tended to rant. Anyway, one day I was going on about how the government was corrupt top to bottom, and only a revolution could ever fix the problem. I had a flair for dramatic statements whenever I talked politics, and it wasn't unusual for me to utter phrases like revolution, and nuke em' all in those days. Most people would just roll their eyes and ignore me, but he surprised me by asking a question. His voice became low and serious, and asked me what if it was possible?

"I was caught off guard, but instead of dismissing his statement I discussed it with him. I stated the obvious, that in this age of technology it would be impossible to start an insurrection without the Government knowing. I also pointed out that the military technology was far too advanced to fight against, and that nothing but a senseless act of terrorism that hurt innocent civilians would be accomplished. He asked me if I would support a revolution that could be accomplished without every firing a weapon. I told him I would, but that would be impossible. I will never forget his reply."

Obviously at this point Doc had us at the edge of our seats, and we urged him to keep going.

"He told me that not only was it possible, but it was already underway, and that was why our research was so important. I had no idea how a failed cure, and a mutated virus we could not control could be the beginnings of a revolution, and I told him so. That's when he told me that it was not the disease but the cure that had mutated, and that figuring out why would be the key to changing the world. This of course had me more confused than before. He leaned in close and kept his voice low as he told me the rest. To sum it up, several of the higher ranking members of the corporation were part of a secret organization that also included people in pretty high positions in the Government, and not just ours."

"Doc, that sounds…"

"Crazy? Yes I thought so too, but look around Jacob, crazy is a daily part of our lives now. He asked his question again, but rephrased. He said 'Hypothetically speaking, if there was a way to end the wars, and the conspiracies, terrorism, poverty, hunger, national debt, taxes, the welfare system, pretty much everything you hate about government; if I held out to you a reset button on our world, would you press it?' I imagine my face looked much like yours do now, and he decided not to continue.

"He told me to forget it, but I couldn't. I tried a few times to get more information from him, but he just said he had made a mistake, and I wasn't ready. He made me swear to never repeat our conversation, or tell anyone he was the one who gave me this information. I tried asking questions of other researchers without raising too much suspicion, but was met with cryptic answers if any. Soon after that my friend transferred facilities and I never saw him again. I decided to leave the facility and help as best as I could out here."

Jacob and I took this all in and tried to process it. I couldn't help thinking that we sounded like a group of teenagers telling scary stories around a campfire, but I couldn't debate that some pretty crazy things had been happening lately. Events I never would have believed if I had not seen them myself. It may have been out of a longing for someone to blame for my wife's death other than God or myself, but I decided that I believed Doc. "What was the name of the society?"

"They called themselves "The Sons of Heaven"; I believe it is a Bible reference."

"It is." Jacob interjected. "A pretty ominous one. Interesting they picked it."

"How so?" I asked

"It refers to Genesis 6:4 which talks about giants who walked the earth in ancient times. It calls them the sons of God, or sons of Heaven, depending on your translation. They have kids with the daughters of men, and these kids become mighty men of renown. One school of thought is that sons of Heaven would refer to angels, and their children would be more or less the superheroes of their day."

"So the treatment is this society's way of making us all, what, demigods? Obviously that plan has backfired a little."

"That's what is so ominous about them picking that verse. The word for giants is naphalim or more literally translated "fallen ones" in the original Hebrew. The school of thought my pastor subscribed to was that these were fallen angels, or demons. I think the name is actually quite appropriate in that light."

All of three of us stayed silent for a minute or two before Jacob again broke the silence. "It sure is a lot to take in isn't it?"

"Yes it is." And after another brief pause. "A biker who speaks Hebrew?"

Doc roared with laughter and Jacob rolled his eyes. "Oh for crying out loud! Ya I'm a biker and I went to church regularly, it was a church of bikers actually. The pastor was a biker too, if you care, and in the course of studying the scriptures we looked at the original translations from time to time. I may have picked up a little Hebrew in the process okay? I'm the biker scholar apparently, I know some Greek too ya jerks."

This got Doc tearing up with laughter, but the lighter mood only lasted so long. I finally had some of the answers, and it only made me hunger for more. I wanted to believe there was more to the story, I needed someplace to aim my anger, but in the end all we had was a bizarre question, and some rumors. We needed more information, and we thought we knew were to get it.

Doc and I decided that we would have to part company with Jacob's caravan, and search for answers at the other research facilities. It was a long shot but maybe we could convince someone to talk, or break in and find the evidence ourselves.

We didn't have much of a plan, but we had to do something, and the facilities seemed to be where the answers were. Our plan was to accompany Jacob's caravan into the sister cities of Palmdale and Lancaster. We would help him disseminate the supplies to the local churches, and then we would head to the National Guard Armory in East Palmdale that had been converted to a treatment facility. Then he would go south back towards L.A, and Doc and I would continue north to the next facility at Edwards Air Force Base together. That was the plan anyway.

12

It was bitter cold, just like that night. I could see my breath coming out in billowed clouds, and the wind felt as if it was rushing straight through my bones. I was standing again in front of an abandoned electronics store. The display TVs in the front window were playing some predictable romance movie. The bride walked down the aisle in her flowing white gown, smiling at her true love and preparing to live happily ever after. I stood there hating that movie. Tears ran down my face as I spoke "I can't do this, how could I? You are my wife!"

I turned from the televisions and looked back at my wife. Her red hair was blowing in the cutting wind and her face was flush from the cold. She looked at me with the kind eyes I remember still, and spoke softly, trying to hold back the emotion in her voice as she removed her ring and leaned forward to slip it into my pocket. She kissed me and held me close one last time.

She took a step back keeping her hands on both my shoulders as she looked deep into my eyes. "You will do what you have to do, because you are my husband, you are stronger than you even know, and I love you very much."

I looked down weeping and ashamed. I was holding my knife in the open palm of my right hand. My wife tenderly put her hands over mine and closed my fingers around the handle, and then let her hands fall away. The knife turned red in my hands, which were covered in blood, her blood.

It was everywhere, my hands, my clothes, the ground. My whole world seemed to be bleeding, even the shadows. The darkness on the ground began to bubble up like boiling water. I watched in horror as out of the boiling shadow shot hands made of the same darkness. The hands grabbed me and pulled me down into the shadows. I screamed into the blackness "What can I do?" The phantom hands pulled me slowly into the shadows.

As the darkness washed over me and I began to drown in it I kept screaming "What can I do? What can I do? What can I do?" I could hear voices screaming in the darkness, crying out for help. I didn't recognize them but somehow I knew that they were all the people I had failed to save along the way. I continued my futile pleading. "What can I do? What can I do?

I woke up sweating, and it took me a few moments to realize where I was. I began to cry silently at the resurfaced memories of my wife, and it took several hours for me to force myself back to sleep. This was the first of many nightmares to come.

13

Up to this point I have only described one attack from the Haunted. This isn't because we only encountered one, but because none of those attacks were very pertinent to my story. I can assure you though that we had already dealt with more than our fair share. We had suffered only small casualties at this point. I am sure it sounds callous to say, but after the amount of death I had seen losing only five people seemed like a good number.

As we moved north some from the group would leave, and more would be added from the surrounding towns and cities that we passed through. By the time we made it to Palmdale we had sixty five people in our caravan.

We had to constantly stop and refuel the larger vehicles, which meant siphoning gas from the abandoned vehicles left along the road, and this got tougher in the smaller cities with less traffic. Troubles also changed regarding the Haunted themselves. In the larger cities they are in a higher concentration, but that doesn't always make it worse.

There is no herd mentality with the Haunted. They don't amble about in groups, becoming hostile only when they smell fresh brains. These creatures have a heightened level of aggression and hostility at all times. Long and short of it is that they don't play well with others, even other Haunted.

There were times when the hordes were so overwhelming that we had to abandon some vehicles and supplies just to escape, but other times they fought amongst themselves so much they barely noticed us.

The Haunted in smaller cities like Palmdale were a different story. The city was very spread out, so the concentration of Haunted was also spread thin. This allowed us to concentrate sixty plus guns on a handful of Haunted at a time, and as flat and treeless as the terrain was we had them spotted quickly; however this also meant we were firing at fewer targets instead of into a crowd, and since they had plenty of open space they maneuvered better than the Haunted in Los Angeles.

In fact it seemed like they were purposefully dodging our fire, whereas the Haunted in Los Angeles tended to make a straight line for us. Because of the spacing we had almost a steady stream of Haunted, sometimes for hours.

We kept to Jacob's usual playbook, and drove the bus into a centralized location on the main highway running through the town. We usually tried to find an elevated section of road, and took the more maneuverable trucks and motorcycles into the actual city streets. We left a group of twenty five with the supplies on the bus, and took the rest into the city. I could tell Jacob never liked splitting the groups up, but we couldn't risk losing the rest of our supplies while we made deliveries, and twenty five guns on that bus could hold for quite a while.

The bus was of course modified to the point where it was an armored vehicle even the military would be proud of, and the elevated road provided choke points of a sort on either side. Our group of motorcycles, and trucks, were still enough to be noticed, but we could maintain a far better speed without the war bus, as I liked to call it.

In the residential areas the Haunted were even more formidable. There were trees and shrubbery in these areas, not to mention the houses, which the Haunted might use as cover. I always laughed at the site of all these transplanted trees and greenery in the middle of a barren desert wasteland. We managed to make it more or less unscathed (a Haunted managed to throw one of the men from his bike, but luckily the bike was the only thing we lost), and moved on to the sister city of Lancaster.

The next day we followed the same routine, bringing supplies to the churches, and stopping at a wholesale food warehouse to trade weapons to the group occupying it in exchange for, well, wholesale foods at discount prices. There was a bit of a shootout at one of the church groups that was located in a Christian School. We had some trouble there with a local gang trying to capture our supplies, but we suffered no casualties. On day three the caravan turned around and headed back to Palmdale to take Doc and me to get some answers.

The building was a fairly plain looking two story done in red brick with a severely faded paint job on the roof, and the American flag flying above the California State flag out front. There was a much larger building and parking lot behind it that had been the actual armory, and a firing range I think, but had been outfitted as medical facilities after the corporation moved in.

The area around the building was nothing but dirt and cracked concrete, but across the street was a beautiful green park, further demonstrating the odd balance of dirt and greenery in this city.

The area looked abandoned and desolate, and the building matched. We saw no apparent security, but approached with our hands raised in surrender, hopefully showing any trigger happy guards that we meant no harm.

Doc stepped forward to talk to them first. We figured he stood the best chance of gaining entrance. As he approached the door I glanced at his face, and saw a look of puzzlement. I followed his gaze to the door, and realized what he was looking at. The door was open just a crack, imperceptible at first, but noticeable as we got closer. Doc walked up, and pushed the door open. It swung slowly and showed us a deserted room. Our hands went from above our heads to holding our weapons, and Jacob signaled for five of his men to join us as we entered the room.

14

The room was dark except for the sunlight leaking through the doorway. I found switches on the wall and flipped them. The lights slowly flickered on casting a pale glow over the rows of cubicles. The room was an open collection of partitioned desks and filing cabinets on the right, with a hallway to the left. We spread out across the room and moved slowly forward through the cubicle labyrinth. When we were satisfied that it was clear we made our way back towards the hallway.

We did our best SWAT team impression as we went through the hallway, four men on each side. There were four offices, two to a side, with closed doors. We put two men on each door and opened them simultaneously to find no one home. We did find makeshift laboratories in the rooms though.

There were files and notes strewn about the desks. Each room had microscopes and vials and other laboratory equipment. To be honest I had no idea what was in there, but Doc looked like he was a kid at Disneyland, before it got overrun of course, so we left him to do his thing while we cleared the second story. In the front of the room was an open spiral staircase that led up to the second story. We made our way up, and began searching the top floor.

The top floor was set up similar to the first floor, but there were no partitions between the desks. The desks also looked much nicer, although they were also littered with scientific gizmos and medical gadgets that I couldn't even begin to describe properly.

I assumed that the armory building was also used as a makeshift medical facility, but never did check. Much like the bottom level, the second level had an open area with multiple desks, and a hallway leading to offices. But this level was smaller than the ground floor, and the hallway was in the back.

This hallway also led to four offices, but now we only had seven men so we went two to a door and I went solo. We opened the doors at the same time and again found no one. The setup in these offices was different than downstairs, and I called out to see if anyone had found the same as me. All three groups answered in the affirmative.

There was a metal rack with several shelves, and each shelf was filled with electronics and cables and a lot of other miscellaneous tech. I knew about as much about the computer stuff we found in those offices as I did about the medical crap we found in the offices on the first floor. On the desk were four monitors, and each had a feed running from what seemed to be traffic cameras at different intersections in the city.

"Looks like Doc isn't crazy after all, I got monitors with camera feeds in here." I called out. Each team called out that they had the same. I moved closer to the desk and saw a notebook lying open in front of the monitors. I set my shotgun down, picked up the notebook, and started flipping through it. It was filled with data and observations about the Haunted.

Four monitors each in four rooms didn't seem like a city wide study sample, so I made the assumption that they were using the PCs at the desk workstations as monitors also. I set the notebook down and called out again to the others "Do you think we should take some of these notebooks as a "know your enemy" kind of thing? You never know, we might learn something new."

"I can teach you something new." The voice was low and guttural, and dripping with venom. My blood had run cold and lightning shot up my spine. I reached for the shotgun and tried to bring it up as I turned, but the thing was on me too fast. It slapped the gun out of my hand like I was a child running with scissors, and grabbed me around the throat with other hand.

Effortlessly it threw me against the wall and lifted me off the ground. "I can teach you about us if you like. Did you know we can talk?" It wore an evil smile as it brought its face close to mine. I felt like I was looking into the face of the devil himself. "Some of us can anyway. We can talk, reason, the only thing we can't do is die; but you can, can't you?" The smile got bigger as he lifted me further up the wall.

His grip was crushing. I couldn't breathe or call out for help, I could barely think. My vision narrowed as darkness encroached upon my peripheral and spotted it with bright swimming lights. My hands began twitching, and I managed a few weak punches that made it shake with silent laughter.

"Do you want to know what the most interesting thing about us is?" He let me slide down the wall so that he could lean his face close again, and whispered "We are not the creatures, and we are not the disease, you are. We are the truth; would you like to learn the truth?" I finally collected myself enough to start kicking the wall to make noise. It let out a chuckle "I guess not."

"Is everything okay in there Isaac?" Jacob had heard my kicks in the next room. I heard the door to that office open, and Jacob's footsteps heading towards the room I was in. "Isaac?" The twisted smile on the things face got even bigger, which I didn't think was possible. I realized that I was leading Jacob into a trap.

I desperately tried to cry out and warn him, but all the words were choked out of me before I could form them. I didn't even have the strength to kick the wall anymore. My body was nonresponsive and the world was becoming more vivid as I faded. The creature would soon choke away whatever life remained in me, and then attack Jacob before he had a chance to process what was happening. The doorknob started to turn, but then I heard another sound.

It was Doc heading up the stairs. I heard his voice, but it sounded so far away now. The vivid world was becoming dull and falling away from me. "Hey guys I think I found something! It doesn't come right out and mention the Sons of Heaven, but it comes pretty close."

As soon as he had mentioned the Sons of Heaven the things eyes went wide. It released its grip on me and let me fall to the ground choking. Jacob must have turned his attention to Doc at this point because the door handle had stopped turning. I was on my hands and knees gasping for breath and still unable to call out a warning. The world was rushing back at me, and I was just trying to get my bearings, and some air.

The Haunted stood there mumbling to itself frantically, asking questions and then answering them while pacing back and forth. It was having a conversation with itself. "They know about us? Obviously they know about us, they just said our name. How could they know? It doesn't matter how, just that they do. What do they know? Now that's a good question!" He seemed excited at that, and shouted at the door. "What do you know about us?"

This obviously alerted Jacob who then threw the door open and raised his gun, but not nearly fast enough. The thing leapt threw the doorway and tossed Jacob out of the way like he was a rag doll. It wasn't interested in him or the other men who had heard the commotion and were coming into the hallway guns drawn.

I finally managed to find my voice and screamed "Doc! It's going for Doc!" It was too fast, and I was too late. I found my shotgun in the corner of the room, and tore through the doorway into the hall. Jacob had managed to get back to his feet and make his way down the hall. He got to the doorway as I was coming through it, and we just barely managed to avoid a collision as we clamored to get to Doc.

Two of Jacob's men had gotten to the top of the stairs ahead of us, but they went no further and hesitated to take the shot. Jacob and I rushed to where they were and saw why. The thing had caught Doc by surprise at the top of the stairs while he was bringing some files up to show us, judging by the papers strewn about. It had caught him and driven him with great force into the pillar that connected to the staircase at about the halfway point.

Doc had indented into the plaster, and there was blood trickling down the wall behind his head. It was pushing Doc against the plaster and screaming in his face "What do you know? What do you know about us?" It was barely an inch from Doc's face, and he looked barely an inch from unconsciousness. Any shot risked going through the creature and hitting Doc, so we held our fire.

The Haunted pulled him back from the wall and then violently slammed him against it again. "Do you know the truth? Do you know why they made us? How many know the truth? Tell me what you know!" I could barely make out words at this point; its questions had become more a demonic growl than actual words.

It slammed Doc against the wall again, and he lost the fight to remain conscious. His head rolled forward lifelessly and his chin rested against his chest. The Haunted made a sort of grunting sound and said with disgust "useless little worm."

I had already started down the stairs screaming in fury. I don't know what I hoped to accomplish against a monster that had recently handled me like a child's plaything, but it did not matter anyway. He shouted "I'll show you all the truth!" and sent Doc's limp body hurtling into the cubicle labyrinth where it landed with a loud crash.

I was halfway down the stairs when it threw Doc, and as I slammed on the brakes and pulled the shotgun up, the others took aim and we lit that thing up. When it saw we had it dead to rights it grabbed the rail of the staircase and quickly hurdled over and down to the floor, but not before I spread its jaw all over the stairs. Jacob and his men also managed to hit it before it escaped, but most of the shots hit in the neck and shoulders with a few hitting the face, but missing the brain.

We all looked over the rail and spotted the creature where it had fallen, and had broken one of its legs. It started limping along for a few steps as we opened up our second barrage of gunfire, but quickly fell into a full sprint after the bone healed itself. My shotgun was useless at this range so I started towards Doc. Though Jacob and the boys managed to hit the Haunted several times they had no more luck from a distance as they had up close up. It bolted past the front door, grabbing it and slamming it as it went by, and disappeared into the maze.

The others kept their weapons up and moved to Doc and me while keeping the weapons trained in the direction of where they last saw the creature. Doc had crashed through a desk nearly fifteen feet from the stairs he was thrown from. He had been pretty banged up even before he was tossed practically across the room, and now there was a sizeable patch of blood on the desk where his head had made contact.

The others had made a protective circle around Doc and Jacob asked how he was doing. I responded shakily "I don't know, I mean he's got to have some broken bones, and the back of his head is matted with blood. I would say we need to grab the Doc but obviously that is not an option here. He's unconscious but alive right now, and his breathing is steady, so the way I see it killing that monster is priority one."

As if on cue we heard a loud crash overhead, and glass and plastic rained down on us. The Haunted had apparently smashed the light above us. Something flew through the air on our left and took out another light. We all aimed in the direction the object had come from, but the Haunted was staying below the cubicles to keep us from having a line of sight. Soon another object flew, and then another, and another.

As the lights shattered one by one it dawned on us what was happening. "It's killing the lights so it can take us in the dark." I said as the remnants of another light fell to the ground.

15

The windows of the building had been closed up long ago making the front door the only source of outside light. As far as I knew the Haunted could not see in the dark any better than us, but without light we had pretty much no chance at a headshot, and if it got in the middle of our group it would be all over.

Another light crashed down as the room plunged that much further into darkness. We could not leave Doc but we were almost out of lights, and we had to do something or we would lose any chance we had of making it out of that building. Shots rang out as some of the men blindly fired into the cubicles. We could hear the thing moving around, but it was too fast and clung to cover too much for any of us to draw a bead.

"Save your bullets, you're not gonna get a clear shot, not yet anyway. We need a strategy, anybody got any bright ideas?" Jacob waited for a reply, but none came. Another light crashed to the ground during the pause, and finally one of his men spoke up.

"We need to get that front door open and get some light, and then we can get some more guys in here and take that thing out."

His name was Frank, but Tank is what Jacob called him. He was a big kid, six foot two and muscular. His head was shaved, except for a stripe of hair right down the middle. He had been an enforcer with a real bad attitude in Esau's gang, but like so many he had his life changed by the bible thumping biker, and left to join Jacob's group. He was a very outgoing guy when I met him, a little goofy, but great to be around.

"That thing is smarter than the other Haunted, and it has us in a pretty good trap." I interjected. "If we split up our numbers we weaken both groups, and run the risk of it taking one of them out. If we move together for the door we'll be slowed by carrying Doc, but I won't leave him behind to be killed. I can stay with him while you guys make a run for it."

"Not needed, I will make a run for the door alone, and you guys stay here."

"Shut up, nobody is sacrificing themselves today you hear me? We are getting out of this together or not at all." Jacob said sternly to us both.

"It's not a sacrifice bossman, when I go for the lights that thing is going to leave its cover to come get me. You guys shoot it before it gets to me. Either we kill it right here or we send it running for cover and we bring in the reinforcements." As he said this one of the other men bent down to tighten his shoelaces. "Doug what are you doing?"

"Tell you what I'm not doing, I'm not pinning our hopes of survival on your running ability 'Tank'. I personally think your plan sucks, but I can't think of a better one. We're almost out of time so I'm going along with it, and since I am the fastest person here white boy, I should be the one doing the running." Doug was about five feet nine, and very thin. He stood in complete contrast to Tank, and was the only one among the five men who wasn't a biker. He was one that

Jacob brought out of the city that had stayed with him, and became one of his most trusted men.

Tank and Doug hated each other at first, and grew close through adversity as men often do. They were like brothers now and often shot racial jokes at each other on account of Doug's being half black and half Asian, and Tank's being a reformed skinhead. Doug called Frank "Cracker" or "White boy", and Frank would fire back with "halfrican", and had taken to calling him the "blazin' Asian" more recently. Doug was extremely fast, as well as being pretty clever, and not half bad with a gun.

Jacob jumped in quickly "Now hold on fellas, we haven't agreed on anything yet. I still say sticking together is our best bet." As he said this more glass cascaded to the ground as yet another light was struck. There were only two lights left, and the darkness had nearly swallowed the room when Doug made the decision for us.

"Sorry boss, we got no time for discussions, I'm going for it." He turned to Frank with a smile. "You just make sure to cover me Honky." With that he took off in a dead sprint for the door and as was expected a shadow came flying out from the cubicle labyrinth at breakneck speed.

Our gunfire lit up the dark room and perforated the shadow as it fell to the ground. If Doug had not stopped, and turned to see how we had done he would have made it to the door. Instead he saw the bullet riddled office chair that had drawn our fire, and uttered a loud curse as the Haunted catapulted itself off of the top of a cubicle.

It leapt half the distance between itself and Doug, and by the time we reacted it was too late. Doug tried to fight it off, but it overpowered him as easily as it had me. It held Doug in front of itself as a shield and began walking towards us. It had its hand wrapped around his throat choking him, and holding him six inches off the ground.

Doug grabbed the things forearm with both hands, pulled himself up to get some air, and yelled at us in choking gasps. "Kill it now! Just shoot it, shoot us both, just KILL IT!" Despite his pleading none of us could pull the trigger, and the creature let out a wicked laugh at our indecision.

"Are you so afraid of bringing death?" It practically snarled at us. "You clutch at your miserable wretched lives as if they are important, as if you are accomplishing something by holding so tightly to something you do not even use properly." It kept walking towards us, carefully positioning Doug to keep us from drawing a bead.

"You spend all your time simply surviving, barely treading water, afraid to drown and become immortal. You are pathetic. Death is freedom. Death is truth. You cannot stop us; the Sons of Heaven will bring truth to the world, and even they do not realize that we are that truth. This world is diseased, and only we can remove the impurities that plague it." It was only steps from us when it stopped and let a twisted smile slowly play across its place. "Would you like to see the truth?"

"I would rather watch you die" Frank had pulled his sidearm and tossed it towards Doug. Doug in one fluid motion caught the gun got his finger on the trigger, and brought the firearm up over his right shoulder to shoot behind him. The monster was once again too fast however, and took its hand away from Doug's throat in a sweeping motion that knocked Doug's hand away just as he squeezed the trigger. It moved with otherworldly speed as it brought its arms up to Doug's head, and with a sickening sound and a bloodthirsty scream snapped Doug's neck. It threw Doug's lifeless body at us to cover itself as it made for the cubicles.

Doug's body had knocked Frank and I to the ground, and caused enough confusion that the Haunted was able to return to cover without any of us getting a shot off. Frank got up, stared at the body of his friend with tears in his eyes, and began visibly shaking from anger.

Without a word he turned and ran into the cubicles. Jacob yelled after him to no avail, and then two more of his men, Martin and George, chased after him yelling for him to come back. Jacob cursed violently; the situation was breaking down quickly. We now had three men chasing the monster recklessly into the maze of office spaces, and three of us standing watch over an injured Doc. Now that we were split up either group would be easy pickings for the creature.

I saw the indecision on Jacob's face. Every instinct in him was telling him to chase after his men, but he couldn't abandon Doc and me either. I spoke up. "I don't want to move him, but we can't stay split up like this, help me get him up."

Jacob took one arm and I took the other as we lifted Doc up and started moving for the cubicles. We let our guns hang by their straps from our shoulders and pulled our side arms. We moved slowly and I didn't like our chances this way, but we were running short on options. Jacob's right hand man Vincent covered us as we made our way towards the others.

We had barely cleared the first cubicle when we heard screams mangled with gunfire and cursing, and finally silence. Vince shot ahead of us, and we got there a few moments after. The scene was carnage and I will not even try to describe it, but Martin and George were most assuredly dead. Frank however was lying on the ground covered in blood holding his gun to the sky and pulling the trigger. He had spent his bullets and so the gun just kept clicking until he threw it to floor in frustration and collapsed.

We set Doc down and Jacob went to Frank. There were punctures all over Frank and blood everywhere. On the floor next to him was what looked to be a letter opener covered in blood. The creature was playing sadistic games with us, killing us for its own amusement.

My knuckles turned white where I was gripping my shotgun as I watched the life drain out of Frank. Finally Jacob bowed his head, placed a hand on Frank and silently prayed before standing back up. "He's gone, let's just kill this thing and get out of here."

I hesitated before stating the obvious "We aren't done here; you know what we have to do."

He let out a sigh of resignation. "I'll take care of Frank, you and Vince take care of George and Martin." We all moved to a body and prepared for our duty. We had to make sure they didn't come back. I was leveling my shotgun at the back of Martin's head when I was startled by a crashing sound, and then another. The last of the lights was gone, and all we had was the faint glow from upstairs, which was not nearly enough.

"No, get away from them!" The Haunted screamed wildly as it jumped into our cubicle. It rushed Jacob and threw him from Frank. Jacob sailed past me and into Vince, sending them both tumbling into the next cubicle. I managed to get my shotgun up and fire at it, but it was already jumping back over the cubicle wall, and I was firing blind into the darkness. I pulled Doc over to where Jacob and Vince were still collecting themselves from off the floor.

"Stay low, we need to make a stand here for a while." A plan was just starting to formulate in my head, but it was far from workable yet.

"We need light is what we need." Vince said. "I can't shoot the thing if I can't see it."

"No kidding, I think that's kind of the point of it taking out the lights in the first place." I said sarcastically. "I think I have got an idea for that though, just try and cover me."

I quickly got up and started turning on computers. We were in the middle of two rows of cubicles, so I started with the Computers on either side of us. I continued down a couple cubicles on each side to give us vision down the row. The computers started up, and went to a login screen, casting an ethereal blue glow across the area. It wasn't much, but it was enough.

We stayed holed up for a few minutes with no sign of the Haunted, not even a sound. "I've never dealt with a Talker before. I've heard stories, but nothing like this." I could hear the undercurrent of fear in Vince's voice. He was unraveling. "I mean talking is one thing. Even it going on about 'showing us the truth' I can deal with, but it strategizes. I mean, it really can think."

Vince was Jacob's friend of almost twenty years, and his most trusted associate. He was a grizzled veteran who had years of experience dealing with trouble, and not just of the undead variety. However I was starting to doubt that he could hold himself together much longer.

Jacob tried in vain to reassure him. "I know it looks bad, but we are going to find a way out of this mess, I promise you that."

"I know, and I trust you with my life Jacob" his voice trailed off.

"But?"

"But this isn't like anything else we have ever faced. We weren't able to save the others, what makes you think we can save ourselves?"

"I honestly don't know Vince, but that doesn't mean that we have the right to give up fighting. That creature murdered my friends, and I do not intend to let that stand. I am going to kill it!"

"But how do you kill something that evil? And we have to do it in the dark no less. How do you kill something like that?"

"You don't." It came from behind me. The Haunted poked its head over the cubicle wall, and gave us a big sadistic smile before disappearing again. We shot up the wall and immediate surrounding area, but when the gunfire ceased we heard its cackling laughter. "You can't stop me, you can't stop the truth. Your friends are learning the truth right now, and when they know it they will teach it to you. It's always better when it comes from a friend." The maniacal laughter was unsettling to say the least.

"The world will soon end, and then begin again. They will make it in their image and make the same mistakes all over again. They will cling to their wretched little lives just as you cling to yours now." The voice kept shifting around the room as it spoke. It sounded like it was coming from where Frank and the others lay.

I heard a slight scraping as if it was picking something up off the ground. "But I know the truth you all hide from. The only true order is in chaos and the only true life is in death. It's time for you to know that truth. It's time to turn out the lights." All we heard after that was the sound of gunfire as it shot up our cubicle. One by one the monitors went dark.

16

I managed to grab one of the monitors off the desk behind me as we all hit the floor. The cord on the monitor was just long enough to let it hang upside down a foot above the floor and act as my flashlight. When the shower of bullets and computers ceased, Vince and Jacob stood up and unloaded in the direction the gunfire had come from, but hit nothing. We could hear its evil laughter as it amused itself with our futile attempts to kill it. I laid my shotgun next to me on the floor and, using the last monitor for light, began searching the drawers of the desk.

Jacob asked me what I was doing and I replied "I think I have an idea, but I need to take a quick inventory. Do you think you two can keep that thing occupied for a few minutes?"

"We'll do what we can. It seems to be content to toy with us until the others start to turn. You know if we stay here too long we are going to be facing our friends as Haunted. We won't survive if that thing gets any help."

"I know, just buy as much time as possible and hopefully I can get us out of here."

I found a few cans of pressurized air, and a dust rag in the first desk. They were useful items, but I needed more. The other desks were much harder to search since I had no light. The whole time the Haunted kept taunting us, rambling on about the truth and waiting for our friends to hear the Call. Jacob and Vince continued to fire in the direction of the taunts, and the creature kept laughing as he dodged the blind shots.

I kept digging around for supplies for my plan, and in desk number four I hit the jackpot. Not only did I find a full container of rubbing alcohol that the previous owner of the desk must have used for cleaning electronics, but for whatever reason there was also a roll of duct tape. There is always hope when you have duct tape.

I put all my newfound treasures in a pile in the middle of the floor, and then grabbed one of the computer towers and threw it to the ground with a crash. As I was pulling it open and scooping out the insides Jacob turned and asked what in the world I was doing. I was working pretty furiously at this point and didn't even look up when I replied almost under my breath "building a bomb."

It is amazing how many things can be used to improvise a bomb. The materials and effects can differ dramatically, but the same basic needs are there. You need a chemical, or gas, or whatever responds to a catalyst by rapidly expanding. You need a container to try to contain the expansion in, and you need that container to fail. You need the catalyst or igniter, and preferably a way to apply that catalyst without blowing your hand off, which usually requires a homemade fuse of some sort.

For my bomb I also needed a way to make it a directional explosive, I used half of the casing for the computer tower I smashed for this purpose. I used the cans of compressed air to provide the rapid expansion and push. A nice combo of other more flammable cleaning sprays, and my shotgun shells would be the catalyst by rupturing the high pressured containers. The rubbing alcohol would provide my liquid fire, and I used it to soak the cleaning rags that would serve as my fuse, and poured a little over my catalysts to insure that my shotgun shells would go off and rupture the compressed air cans.

I broke a hole in the side of the casing to run the fuse through. After I used the duct tape to rig everything into its proper place, I filled the others in on my plan. I was giving it the once over and admiring my handiwork when Jacob addressed me in between taking potshots at the Haunted.

"Are you almost done over there? We are getting severely low on ammo."

"I think it's ready for the field test."

"Will that contraption work?"

"No clue, but I am a glass half full kind of guy, so if it does not work I will be dead anyway, and won't really care anymore."

I stood up, lifted my abomination off the ground, and pulled out my lighter. "Let's do this."

The Haunted was still blathering on when I yelled "I can't take this, I'm going for it" and sprinted, presumably for the door, with my case of goodies in my arms. I expected the Haunted to go for me right away, but it must have sensed another trap.

I had made it halfway to the door without hearing foot steps behind me when I turned around to see where the creature was. I heard a loud crash over by Jacob and Vince, and though it was hard to see in the dark I could make out that there was a desk halfway through their cubicle's wall. The cubicle had collapsed in on Vince and Jacob, pinning them. The Haunted thought we were pulling the same trick as before and used the desk as a distraction this time. The moment I processed all of this through my brain I saw that the Haunted was almost on me.

It leapt through the air and tackled me to the ground, pinning my shoulders, and bringing its sadistic smile close to my face. "I knew you would see the light. It would be better coming from your friends, but since you are so anxious to learn the truth I will show it to you."

The force of it tackling me had knocked my lighter out of my hand, and well out of reach. Luckily the thing did not have my arm completely pinned, and I was able to raise my sidearm, and begin firing it into the monster's stomach. It laughed in my face, reveling in my struggles. It was so busy relishing its victory it did not even notice the bomb sitting on my chest.

The Haunted also didn't realize that I wasn't trying to shoot it, but was trying to use the muzzle flash from my gun to light the fuse. One, two, three, four, five shots fired without it lighting. I was starting to panic, and the creature just kept laughing in my face. "It is useless; you can't fight death, it always wins. Are you ready for the truth?"

It moved its hands to my throat for the kill, and I pulled the trigger one more time. The rag lit up and burned its way quickly into the bomb. The Haunted was startled and loosened its grip on my throat as it looked on. I had dropped my gun and was using both hands to hold the bomb in place. The flame from my fuse gave enough light for me to watch the mixture of confusion and even fear creep onto the things face. A wicked smile was creeping onto mine, and I said "Truth is I'm ready to watch you burn."

The explosive gave a load pop and hiss, and slammed the case back into my chest as the flaming liquid spewed out. The heat rushed over my face making it near impossible to breath. My fingers were badly burned but the rest of me was fine. The Haunted shrieked in pain, the makeshift office claymore had done even better than I had hoped.

The Haunted was stumbling backwards completely aflame. None of this was enough to kill it of course, but that was not the plan. My job was merely to stun it. Jacob and Vince had managed to evade its earlier attempt to crush them with the desk, and were running out from the cubicles to finish the job.

One of my pant legs had caught fire, and I was busy putting it out when I heard the shot. I think it was Vince who put the thing down, but I could be wrong. In any case the thing fell lifeless to the ground missing most of its head.

It was not over yet unfortunately. I went to check on Doc while Jacob and Vince went about the grim task of making sure our dead friends stayed dead. When I went to Doc I was surprised to see his eyes open. He was struggling to speak and I leaned closer. "Did you get it?"

"Ya Doc, we got it."

"Did it get us?"

I nodded my head and tried to control my voice "Everybody but me, you, Jacob, and Vince."

"I think it is going to get me too. My ribs feel like mush, and I have lost blood. Probably have internal bleeding and a concussion to boot."

"Don't talk like that; you are going to make it Doc. Can you stand?"

"I think so, with some help."

I helped him get to his feet. He put an arm around my shoulders, and I helped him walk towards the others who were waiting at the door. Doc muttered something weakly.

"What was that Doc?"

"Edwards." His words were pained, like someone was twisting a knife into his gut. "Edwards Air Force Base."

"What about it?"

"I think the people behind everything are at the research facility at Edwards called Phillips Laboratory."

"How did you figure that out?"

"I'll explain it later; I just wanted to tell you before I pass out again or, you know, die."

"Stop talking about dying or I'll kill you myself."

He smiled weakly at that, and we joined the others at the door. They were excited to see Doc awake, and Jacob grabbed Doc's other arm to help me carry him. Vince grabbed for the door.

"I bet they are all wondering what took us so long. It is kind of odd no one came in after us though." As Vince said this he was reaching for the door, and we could hear gunfire coming from outside. "It sounds like they are having some Haunted problems themselves. Probably just a few more wanderers." He opened the door.

We stepped through the door into the blinding light to see what was happening outside. Instantly we knew why no one came to check on us. It was a war zone.

17

Bodies littered the ground. Human and Haunted alike were intertwined in the blood and debris. The survivors from our group were all holed up in the bus firing an avalanche of bullets into the crowd of Haunted. There was a crowd attacking the bus, with a few stragglers milling about the area. The concentration of Haunted was more than I would expect in one place in a small city. We had no chance of reaching the bus through the horde, and we were low on ammo from our confrontation, so we headed for the nearest cover we could find.

There was an abandoned sedan in the little lot on the side of the building. It would provide cover while still being close enough to help thin the crowd of Haunted. We collected weapons and ammo from some of the bodies as we went. When we reached the sedan we leaned Doc up against it, and then got set up to start shooting.

"Hey Isaac, what do you make of that?" Jacob asked pointing towards the bus.

I had not noticed it before, but several of the guy's motorcycles were piled up in front of the bus. The Haunted were climbing up them to get to the windows, and then falling back down as our people took them out. They were holding them back well but every Haunted they took down just added to the pile of scrap metal and mangled corpses, and allowed more Haunted to climb up towards the windows.

Two of the Haunted were rolling one of the trucks to the back of the bus. We heard crunch of metal as they flipped it onto its side. "What in the world are they doing?" Then as if in answer to my question they both took several steps back from the wreckage and raised automatic rifles. "Are they doing what I think they are doing?"

"Take them out!" Jacob exclaimed as they began peppering the bottom of the truck with bullets. All three of us were practically synchronized as we brought up our rifles, rested them on the sedan, and fired on the two Haunted.

One was a petite woman, not more than five feet tall, and dressed in a military uniform. The other was a tall broad shouldered man in civilian clothes. The first shots were rushed and though we scored some hits we were unable to kill either one of them, but we did manage to get them to stop shooting the truck at least.

The man quickly dove for cover behind the nearest vehicle. The woman, in an amazing show of agility, climbed atop the truck with ease. She ran across the top of the bus and jumped to a light post, then to a flagpole and finally to the roof. When she was on the roof we lost sight of her, but she soon peered over the edge and began firing.

The shots were fired almost blindly as if she was merely pinning us down. We moved to the rear of the vehicle. Jacob and I fired back at the girl while Vince continued to fire on the man, who was still pinned down across from the truck he was attempting to set on fire.

"Guys, I have to get to that male Haunted or he is going to try and cook everyone on that bus. If I make a run for it can you two keep the girl…"

Before he could finish she came leaping from the top of the building. She was much more graceful, and much quicker than the talker we had faced inside. She landed on the trunk in a slide that brought her feet into Jacob who was directly in front of her and sent him flying. She grabbed Vince and I by the throat as she continued the slide and used her momentum to throw us forcefully to the ground.

I was getting real tired of being tossed around by these things, and quickly rolled out of the way and came up with my gun raised. Vince and Jacob had also made it back up with their guns at almost the same time. We had managed a little separation from the Haunted and positioned ourselves evenly on three sides of her.

There would be no escape this time. Unfortunately, while we were rolling to our feet, she had grabbed Doc and was holding a knife to his throat. We hesitated, unsure of what was going to happen next, when she spoke.

"You should not interfere; we are only trying to help you all." Her voice was soft, barely more than a whisper, almost frail sounding. It was more like the voice of a shy child, but also emotionless, and detached sounding. "Why do you fight us when we are only trying to save you?" She could not have been much older than twenty, with raven black hair and big dark brown eyes. She had slightly pointed features in her face, and fair skin. She was likely beautiful once, but now had the same soulless, inhuman look that they all possessed.

She had Doc on his knees, and was holding his head up by a fistful of his hair, holding the knife so that the tip drew a small bead of blood from his neck. "You are all diseased, slowly decaying and clinging to existence. You know pain and sorrow every day. You think you can change that, but you can't. Life is sorrow and loss until you embrace death's sweet release." A small smile crept across half of her face. "I can release you from your prison"

That wicked smile told me we were coming up on the end one way or the other, and I was trying to figure out what our best move was. She had her face right next to Doc's and these things were just too fast to try and take a shot. Doc's hand was inching towards the holster carrying his sidearm, but I knew that would be a mistake.

Doug had not been fast enough to do it, and Doc was not in any condition to be fast. I just hoped he realized that too. He did, and yelled out at us "I am dying anyway, just shoot us both!" But just like with Doug I knew none of us could pull the trigger. As the Haunted's smile spread to the other side of her face Doc went for his gun. "Fine, I will do it myself." Quicker than I thought he could still move he pulled his gun, held it to his own chest, and pulled the trigger.

The selfless move stunned the Haunted as well as us. She stumbled back and let Doc's limp body fall to the ground, the smile growing larger. The hole in her own chest was already closing as she spoke excitedly. "Do you see now? Your friend is ..." The Gunfire from our three weapons drowned her out. As her body fell we were already running to Doc. He was still breathing, and even still conscious.

He smiled and struggled as he spoke. "See that wasn't so hard was it?" I could not help a small half laugh at that, but then urged Doc not to speak. "Don't worry; I don't think I hit anything vital. I am a doctor after all."

"Not even you can perfectly predict the path of a bullet through your chest Doc, and as you yourself have said, you're just a Physician's Assistant."

He laughed at that, but then winced in pain. I apologized for making him laugh, and told him again to stop talking and save his strength while we got busy trying to stop the bleeding. I took off my shirt and ripped it in half to use to apply pressure to both wounds, since the bullet had gone straight through.

Jacob took over applying pressure and spoke to Doc. "Doc, I know you and I go round and round on the subject of faith, but if you do not mind I would like to talk and pray with you."

Doc let out another pained laugh and replied. "I actually can't think of anything I would like better, but you guys are not done yet." Doc was pointing towards the bus, and we looked to see that the other Haunted had succeeded in starting a fire. "Go save the others, I promise I won't die until you get back." Reluctantly we left Doc there and ran back to help the others.

The truck they had been trying to ignite earlier was now aflame, but also several of the motorcycles piled around the bus had caught fire. By the time we got over there the bus was nearly engulfed, and the door was blocked by burning motorcycles and Haunted corpses.

We did not see the Haunted that was starting the fires in the immediate vicinity, and the people in the bus were our first priority, so we starting looking for a way to evacuate them. The front of the bus was pretty much clear of fire so we decided that would be our exit point.

Vince and Jacob helped me up the hood and I got to work breaking and raking the glass of the front windshield. They went one to each side of the truck picking off the stray Haunted that the bus firing squad had missed. The heat was pretty intense, and the people in the bus were pretty happy to see me.

They were choking on smoke, and looked pretty haggard, but they seemed more or less physically okay. I had just started pulling the first one out when I heard a maniacal sounding voice "You may want to stand back." I let go of the person I was pulling out of the bus, grabbed my gun and stood up. There on the roof of the bus, not five feet from me was the male Haunted who had started the fires.

I have mentioned earlier that I have only seen three Talkers in my travels. I suppose I neglected to mention that I met them all in the same day. He was crouched down, and as I raised my gun he leapt forward and grabbed it by the barrel, keeping it pointed away from him. I froze, I was pretty sure it was about to kill me when it leaned forward and smiled at me.

"Like I said, you may want to get back." As he said this he was tossing a small round object up and catching it like a baseball. He stopped tossing it and held it up for me to see. It was a grenade. "This is about to get messy." He flicked the pin free from the grenade with his thumb, and tossed it through the windshield into the bus, then let go of my gun and leapt from the bus.

18

The grenade bounced off the driver's seat headrest, and under one of the bench seats. I was frantically screaming "Grenade, grenade! Everybody get to the back!" One of the men dove for the grenade attempting to smother it, but after he fished it out from the seat there was no time, and he was not able to cover it completely. He was an ex Marine named Sam, and though he wasn't able to save everyone, his act limited the damage and deaths. Unfortunately the handful of people around him, and myself perched precariously on the hood, were too close. The force of the blast hurled me through the air in a burst of heat, shattered glass, and blood.

The pavement rushed up to greet me, and I landed on my right side dislocating my shoulder. The glass remnants cut into my hands as I struggled back to my feet. I began a sort of drunken stumble back towards the bus. I could hear Jacob screaming with the kind of anguish that only a leader who's seen those he protected taken away in one single violent act can experience.

He was sprinting towards the front of the bus with reckless abandon. He was so concerned with checking for survivors that he was oblivious to the talker that was stalking him. It had climbed back on the roof of the bus walking along it with its eyes fixed on Jacob, and a smile fixed on its face.

I was ambling along still not recovered from the blast. I wanted to call out but instead had to stop and fall to my knees while apparently trying to cough out a lung. I caught my breath as best I could and tried to force myself to get moving again. Even if I had managed to warn Jacob I doubt he would have heard me, he was solely focused on his people in that bus. As he grabbed for the front of the bus, to pull himself up, the Haunted broke into a run and was headed in for the kill.

I managed to find my feet and began to run towards Jacob, but there was no way I could reach him in time. At that moment Vince came around from the other side of the bus with his weapon raised and trained on the Talker. While the Talker had been stalking Jacob, Vince had been stalking it.

He shot in controlled bursts, with the first shots hitting the chest, then the neck, and as the creature leapt towards him he put a couple practically right in the things mouth. The bullet sprayed a mist of blood out the back of its head, and destroyed its front upper teeth, and half its nose. He had failed to hit the brain however, which is the shot that matters, and soon the thing had leapt on him and pinned him to the ground.

My right arm was still hanging useless and too weak to hold a weapon. I pulled my sidearm with some difficulty, and transferred it to my left hand. After the Talker threw Vince to the ground with force he turned and quickly disarmed Jacob before he could even fire a shot.

It smashed Jacob into the metal grill of the bus, and then tossed him off to the side effortlessly. I managed to land a few shots in the things chest but shooting left handed I had no chance of killing it. Jacob's gun was lying at its feet. It kicked the gun up, and caught it out of the air. It sprayed fire at my legs, and when I went down turned from me disinterested.

It walked back over to Vince who was just starting to recover from having his head bounce off the pavement like a basketball. It simply picked him up over its head, walked over to the still burning vehicles, and threw him into the fire. Jacob and I were both still on the pavement looking on in horror. Vince let out a scream that I still hear in my nightmares. I was crawling on the pavement towards the thing, blood streaking the ground behind me. I don't know what I thought I was going to do, but I wanted this nightmare to end one way or the other.

The Talker walked slowly in my direction, that sadistic smile they all wear playing once more across its face. It stopped at the front of the bus, and looked sideways at the horizontal metal bars that made up its grill. Its smile got bigger as it grabbed one of them and bent it outwards. One end snapped completely free, and it bent it until it formed a sort of makeshift spike. It walked over to me, picked me up, and drove me onto the spike until I could see a good foot of it sticking out my chest.

I will not try to describe the pain to you simply because there are not words. I screamed and retched in pain, and then began slipping in and out of consciousness. I saw the thing toying with Jacob, knocking him to the ground, and kicking him violently. It dragged him in front of me and made him watch the life pour out of my chest. It began talking about showing me the truth I think, but by this time its voice sounded distant as I slipped between worlds.

Regret washed over me as I fell into darkness and the cold pierced through me. It was bitter cold, just like that night. It was my nightmare again, but this time even more real. The hands grabbed me and pulled me into the shadows, and again I heard the voices calling to me. I recognized them this time. Doug, Doc, George, Martin, Frank, and so many others I had failed to save.

The hands held me and made me gaze down on Jacob as if I was looking at another world. The Talker was holding him by the throat with one hand and laughing at his conquest. The voices cried out for me to do something, but I was so powerless. I screamed "What can I do!" The phantom hands pulled me slowly into the shadows.

As the darkness washed over me and I began to drown in it I kept screaming "What can I do? What can I do? What can I do?" I looked down at my hands holding the knife, and then up at my wife standing before me. Her red hair blowing in the cutting wind and her face flush from the cold. "What can I do? You are my wife!"

She looked at me with the kind eyes I remember still, and spoke softly trying to hold back the emotion in her voice as she removed her ring, and leaned forward to slip it into my pocket. She kissed me and held me close one last time. She took a step back and, keeping her hands on both my shoulders she looked deep into my eyes. "You will do what you have to do, because you are my husband, you are stronger than you even know, and I love you very much."

I looked down weeping and ashamed. The knife turned red in my hands. My hands were covered in blood, in her blood. It was everywhere, my hands, my clothes, the ground. My whole world seemed to be bleeding, even the shadows.

The darkness bled over everything until there was nothing but blackness. I kept staring at my hands but the knife and blood were gone, replaced by the metal sticking out of my chest. "What can I do?" I said sobbing. "What can I do?"

I looked up and my wife was standing with me in the blackness. She looked at me, but not with the eyes I remembered, they were cold vindictive eyes. She leaned close and whispered in a voice that still makes me shudder when I recall it "Kill them Isaac, kill them all."

19

Anger washed over me like the afternoon sun. It burned away all of my despair and replaced it with desire for vengeance. I wanted vengeance on the Sons of Heaven for using us as pawns in their chess game, and on anyone who helped develop this cursed treatment; the scientists studying us like rats while they hid away taking notes on how we turn. Were they watching as I was forced to murder my own wife?

I could feel the hate building in my chest like a stoked fire as I thought about it. Images were flashing by of all the friends I had lost, of the Haunted that butchered us, and of the Talkers who taunted us. I could see Doc lying on the ground bleeding to death, Vince's burning remains, and Jacob kicking at the air struggling to breathe as the Talker choked him to death.

I opened my eyes and breathed in deep, filled with a new purpose. I was going to make every last one of them pay. I would show them, up close and personal, the monster they had unleashed on us. But first I was going to save my friends. I stepped forward slowly, the metal sliding through my skin with a sickening sound.

I was too enraged to care about the pain anymore. I could feel my blood pumping and the adrenaline kicking in as my field of vision narrowed to include only the Talker who was killing my friend.

It heard my steps behind it and turned to see who was approaching. When it saw me walking towards it, my wound closing and healing as I went, it let Jacob fall to the ground, and smiled at me like I was an old friend. "You have seen the truth! Now you know how meaningless it is to fi…"

"Why won't you just shut up?" My scream interrupted the things celebration. I rushed it with speed I never had before, and grabbed the stunned Haunted by the throat, lifting it slowly into the air. The look in its eyes had turned from confusion to fear as it realized that I meant to kill it, and I now had the ability to succeed. I threw it back towards the front of the bus.

When it stood up I saw that the look in its eyes had turned bloodthirsty. It flew at me and I rushed to intercept. My rage fueled me as the blows came so fast my mind could not keep up. I was moving on predatory instinct and rage, and had soon overpowered the Talker, pinning it to the ground where it seethed at me behind a mask of hate.

I started to smile as I spoke. "You don't seem very talkative all of a sudden." The creature breathed heavily, practically spitting its anger through barred teeth. "Now that you've finally shut up, I think I miss the sound of your voice." I was giving in to the madness, and enjoying every second. "I know what I can do to get you talking again. You like to talk about truth a lot, how about I show you the light?" With that I grabbed the Talker, turned and threw him into the fire near Vince's still burning corpse.

I jumped into the fire, and onto the Talker. He screamed horrifically as I held him in the flames, and let them engulf us. The Haunted heal almost instantaneously, but they still feel pain. His body was regenerating tissue only to have it burn away again as I held it there and began bludgeoning its face. I felt the bones in my hand break and then heal as I transferred all my rage into those blows. Faces of lost friends flashed through my brain with each one. When my mind stopped on the image my wife's lifeless form I let out an animalistic scream and the blows became more rapid and wild.

Jacob was screaming at me, trying to bring me back from the brink of madness. Some of the others had started to climb out of the bus, and they joined Jacob. Eventually they managed to pull me out of the fire, and off of the Talker. It began to crawl out of the fire, the bones in its face reforming, and skin regenerating as we watched.

I had gotten a hold of myself enough to convince the others to let go of me. Without a word I walked to the pathetic creature, and grabbed it by its newly grown hair. I dragged it to the spike it had hung me on and pressed its miserable head against it. Its jaw had not quite finished reforming, and it struggled as it spoke. "But... the... truth..." I pushed forward and silenced it forever.

20

Sam's sacrifice kept the fatalities on the bus to a minimum, but many were still injured, and many had died who were outside the bus when the initial wave hit. The rest of that night was spent gathering the wounded and moving everyone to one of the churches for protection, and hopefully treatment, while Jacob plotted the group's next steps.

He decided to go to the church in Lancaster. Although it was farther away it had the largest facilities, and he knew several of the congregation who had at least some medical training. The Church facilities had originally been a Christian School, so we brought all the minor injuries into the School's gymnasium and set up our own version of a triage center. The worst injuries were brought to what had once been the nurse's office. This included Doc, who was still hanging on.

For the next three days Jacob and I said nothing about what had happened. He was pretty busy as the group's leader, and I was just worried about Doc. Doc may be the toughest man I have ever had the pleasure of knowing. After three days of touch and go, he appeared to be in the clear. He was still banged up pretty bad, and restricted to bed rest, but didn't seem to be critical. We sat in that room talking about just about everything that was not connected to the current events.

Jacob came in to check on Doc also, and all three of us talked and laughed for at least a couple of hours before we knew it could be avoided no longer. Jacob sighed heavily and began speaking in a tone that held enough gravity in it to let us know we were getting down to business. "Doc, I can't tell you how happy I am that you made it. And that you are feeling better, but there is something you need to know." He turned to me. "Isaac I think it would be best coming from you."

I agreed, and began to tell Doc everything that happened after we left him. It all hit him pretty hard, and his countenance grew solemn as he listened to the death toll. It had not been long since Doc and I first began traveling with this group, but adversity has a way of forging bonds at a much faster rate than you would think. I realized sitting there that we had formed roots with this group, something that was extremely dangerous to do in our situation. When I got to the end his manner became especially grave.

"So you have heard the Call then." It was a statement rather than a question.

"Yes I have, and because of that I think it would be best if I went to Edwards alone. You shouldn't go anyway in your condition, and I obviously don't have the time to wait for your wound to heal." I paused for a moment and let out a heavy sigh. "More than all that though, I don't want to risk turning while any of you are near me."

"So you chose exile? I assumed you would want to try and find the truth before you turned."

"I chose exile" I conceded "but I won't lie to you Doc, I'm going there for more than just truth. I'm looking for revenge."

Jacob jumped in at this point. "As soon as you are ready Doc, I promise I will take you down there myself."

Doc smiled. "Actually I don't want to go anymore. I know it might sound selfish or wrong, but I almost died, and I find that I really don't care why all of this happened or who was responsible. The fact is it did happen, and now we'll probably die because of that. Before I go I want to have a few more discussions on faith with you Jacob, and I want to help this group help as many people as possible. I assume you could use a PA?"

I could not help a laugh. "Doc, I don't think the medical community would mind if we just assume the MD. What are they going to do, come down here and strip you of your license?"

We talked for several more hours. I had found some small measure of happiness in this group, and it would be hard to leave that. But I had discovered enough proof to convince me that someone was responsible for what had happened to my wife. I could not lose this chance to make them see the horror of what they had done. I left Doc and Jacob and went to prepare for my exile.

I should explain our use of the term "exile". As I have mentioned before, one of the problems in forming groups was that we had no clue how the virus was spread. We know now that the treatment is the cause and anyone who received it, which is pretty much everyone, will turn. All we knew back then was that there was no way to predict who would turn, and how fast they would turn. Honestly, I still don't completely understand it. What we did begin to understand was what some of the symptoms were. Groups had to watch closely for the symptoms, and decide what to do with that person if it was suspected they were hearing the Call.

In some groups this meant that person was shot as soon as they showed symptoms. Those who began to have the symptoms would try to hide it for fear of their lives, and that caused distrust among those groups. Some groups would place the person in restraints, feeling it more humane to kill them after they had turned. These groups underestimated the Haunted, and their ability to escape restraints, and quickly died out quite literally. Other groups who did not want to kill, but were not fond of being killed, would leave the person behind unarmed and without provision; this pretty much insured that they would be killed and join the rising number of Haunted. Then there was Jacob.

Jacob's group gave two options. The first was for those who were sure that their soul was at peace. They would gather everyone together to pray over that person. They would sing songs of worship together; then Jacob would teach them from the Bible and say a final prayer for that person before killing them himself. He never let anyone else shoulder that burden.

I do not understand this kind of faith, but I won't lie and say I don't envy it. I wish I had the strength they have, the strength my wife had. As much as I longed to meet my death with peace in my heart there was too much anger there already.

The second way was exile, or as I jokingly referred to it, the long walk. I have a dark sense of humor I know, but I live in dark times. Jacob refused to take the life of anyone who wasn't sure of where they were going, but he also could not risk them turning while still among the group.

They would be given a vehicle, weapons, ammo, and supplies enough to last for a couple weeks, and allowed to leave and find their own peace or truth, or whatever it is they were still looking for. They would also be given a Bible with a few passages marked. It might not seem like much to you reading this, but it was more than most would do for you. I can't call myself a believer, but I do still have that Bible.

It was the next day before I left the group. I will not bore you with the details of my departure, but simply say after many prayers, tears, and words of encouragement, I began my journey towards vengeance.

21

Edwards was only a half hour drive from Lancaster, and I was not intending to go any further than that. I brought barely a week's worth of food and water, and used the bulk of my parting gift for weapons. The vehicle I chose was a silver pickup, and I nearly filled the bed with weapons and ammo. It was more than they should have let me take, but Jacob knew what I would be going up against, and had insisted.

Making my way through the Base, and to Philip's Lab, was going to be difficult. Not only because of the Haunted, but there was the distinct possibility that I would be fighting my way through the Security at the lab as well, But I was determined to get through no matter what it cost me, or what I had to do.

There were few vehicles on the long stretch of road that led to the base, and I was able to drive at a pretty good speed most of the way. Both sides of the long desert highway were bordered by expansive dry lake beds, and very little vegetation aside from the tumble weeds.

In the distance was a collection of hills that had almost a bluish hue to them as they stood against the clear blue sky. The good thing about the vast expanse of flat dirt was that it gave me a clear view for miles. The only things even resembling cover were the Joshua trees, and they were far too spread out and scrawny to provide adequate camouflage. Driving down that empty road with no possibility of a Haunted ambush, I almost felt normal again.

As I neared the base the road curved around a small hill creating the only blind spot that could pose any trouble. I slowed as I approached it, and kept my right hand near the automatic rifle in the passenger's seat.

There were road signs going around the turn. They were faded, but still readable. The first said "If you have been drinking" followed by "and driving" "and have not been caught" "you are about to be" almost immediately after reading the last one the guard shack came into view causing me a chuckle or two. I stopped laughing when I saw the group of Haunted charging at it. There were six of them in the group, but more were already lying on the ground in front of the shack.

I brought the truck to a stop about twenty yards away from the group. The guard shack was more like a small office, and through the glass I could see someone standing just inside the door. I pulled the rifle from the seat, opened my door, and used it to steady the rifle. While I did this I saw that another Haunted had fallen.

Whoever was trapped in there was fighting back. There was a large window on the side down from the door. One of the Haunted was attempting to break it down, but it apparently was bulletproof. It was still making progress though so I concentrated my fire there.

The first shots ran up its back and instantly attracted the attention of the others. I had failed to get a headshot on the one at the window but now had to worry about the four who were charging me. Before I even had a chance to decide whether to try one more time for the one at the window a fine red mist spewed from its head. It painted the window red, which gave me pause because that meant the bullet came from behind, and there was another shooter.

That was a positive development, but my biggest concern at this point was the group of Haunted tearing across the road, and coming right at me. There were four of them now closing the distance incredibly fast. One of them crumpled as it ran, and stained the desert floor with the former contents of its head.

I managed to get a headshot on another, but the other two were on me too fast. The first grabbed the barrel of my gun, and used it to pull me into the door of the truck. The gun slipped from my hands as the other grabbed me, and threw me clear of the truck. I hit the pavement, and rolled to my feet, pulling my knife as the two Haunted came at me from both sides.

I had kept this particular knife with me since I was forced to use it on my own wife. I had stopped using it for a long time, but had brought it back out to remind me of my new goal, to make the people who turned my wife into one of these creatures pay. Even holding it in my hand brought all the pain and hate to the surface where I needed it to be.

I leapt forward into the one on my left, it was clearly surprised by this action and I tackled it pretty easily. When I was able to pin it to the ground with one hand while raising the knife above my head, it looked downright astonished. The other Haunted grabbed me before I could bring the knife down, but I fought out of its grasp, and let loose a front kick to its chest that sent it flying.

I turned back to the Haunted on the ground just as it was scrambling back to its feet, and snapped a low kick at its legs. I connected with its left knee, and heard a sickening pop as it went down on its right knee. A quick knee to its face sent it the rest of the way down, and the knife I buried in its heart made sure it stayed there.

I jerked the knife and felt warm blood splash my face as I turned back to the other Haunted smiling, and falling deeper into the insanity of bloodthirsty hate. It had regained its feet and was lunging at me with a hate filled scream. My instincts had taken complete control, and before I could decide how to counter the knife had already left my hand. It flew end over end and buried itself in the things skull with a loud thud.

I stood there breathing heavily, and tried to control my rage. It seemed that the Haunted strength was only available to me when I was enraged, but each time I went to that place it seemed harder to come back. I knew eventually I would simply surrender to the rage and became Haunted forever, but I had to fight it long enough to reach my goal. I managed to slow my breathing and bring myself under control. My hands were trembling slightly and I closed my eyes and exhaled slowly. That's when I heard the noise behind me.

The problem with stabbing a Haunted in the heart is that it actually does kill it, but not fast enough. It stops the flow of blood, causing the Haunted to enter a deathlike state, but even without blood flow the brain will not die for several minutes. That is unfortunately more than enough time for its heart to heal and begin pumping again. I had made a fatal mistake.

The Haunted had closed in on me unnoticed while I had been regaining my composure, and was too close for me to react in time. The worst part was that I was no longer enraged and therefore no longer a match for its strength. It was positioning its hands to snap my neck, and as I tried to turn towards it I could see it grinning at me over my left shoulder. It had me, and we both knew it. Just as it began to apply the pressure to my neck I heard what sounded like the hiss of air being forced from a compressor, followed by a wet smack.

The body of the Haunted fell lifelessly against my shoulder and slid down leaving a streak of blood down my left side. The sniper was in an observation tower about a hundred feet to the side of the Guard shack, and at least a hundred and fifty feet behind it. There were dishes of some sort on top, probably radar, and an old retired cargo plane had been parked behind it as some sort of tourist attraction.

I waved my thanks to the sniper, retrieved my knife from the Haunted skull it was resting in, and headed towards the shack to check on whoever had been trapped inside. It appeared to be a man dressed in a black tee shirt with a hat pulled low and dark sunglasses. He had not moved from his spot behind the door, and as I got closer I saw why. It was a mannequin.

"That is Manny; he is the strong silent type."

I turned around laughing, and raised my hands to show I meant no harm since he had his rifle trained on me. "Haunted actually fall for that trick?"

He smiled. He was down from his tower and standing fifty feet away. "You actually fell for that trick. Who are you, and what is your business?"

"Thanks for your help, but as I'm sure you already know I'm on a bit of a tight schedule." I started to head back to the truck when his tone gained an almost annoyed tone that I suspected was his attempt at sounding stern.

"Who are you, and what is your business here?" He was in his early twenties, tall and thin with blond hair, light skin, and an almost indifferent manner. He walked closer, keeping his rifle raised, until he was only about forty feet away.

I turned back to face him. "My name is Isaac, and I'm just passing through."

"You need to wait here so that the Commander can come and clear you before you can enter." He said it like he was giving me the time, or discussing the weather. He had closed to thirty feet. His gun was raised but he didn't seem nervous or tense. His manner was calm to the point of boredom.

"I told you, I don't have the time to waste. I have something to do, and not much time to do it."

"What do you have to do?" His hair had fallen forward completely covering his left eye, and he did a poor job at feigning interest.

"It is none of your business."

"I don't really care anyway, just passing time." He sighed heavily to convey his boredom. "I already made the call, they should be here shortly. You can sit down in the office."

"I told you I don't have the time." The irritation was creeping into my voice. I didn't come this far to be delayed, and risk turning before I accomplished my goal. "I am getting in that truck, and driving through this base, and if you don't like it you can just shoot me. You better shoot me in the head though, or you'll just make me angry."

He turned the gun towards the truck, took aim, and fired two shots, one in each tire. He did it so fast that he had the gun trained on me again before I could even react. I could feel the anger rising up again. "I have to get through. I have to get to Philip's Lab, and I have to do it soon." I could barely control my voice at this point.

"You mean the research facility? Why do you want to go there?" He seemed genuinely interested this time, but I did not have the time or patience. All I could think of was how far I had come just to fail. He was only twenty feet away now, and had stopped walking.

"I told you I do not have the time!" I was drowning in a sea of anger and frustration. I made a desperate attempt to reach, and disarm him. After a few long strides I leapt at him like only the Haunted or someone on the verge of becoming one can leap. I cleared ten feet in a single jump, but rather than try to hit a head shot he aimed his rifle low, and put one in my right leg just as I landed on it with most of my weight. It buckled and I went down in a heap.

His tone was razor sharp now. "Don't move. I'm sorry I had to shoot you, but it will heal pretty fast from what I have seen of you. Your head won't heal though, so please stay still." He kept his rifle trained on my head as he backed up a few paces. My anger was turning to anguish. I obviously had no choice but to wait for this "Commander" and try to hang on to my sanity.

"Fine we can play it your way. I think I will take that chair in the Guard Shack after all, unless you are having second thoughts about blowing my head off." He stood there thinking a moment, and then let his gun fall to his side and hang from the strap around his shoulder, then moved it towards his back. I picked myself off the ground. My leg still felt like it was on fire, but the wound had already closed and healed. "You're not afraid of me trying to disarm you again?"

There was a faint click as he undid the strap on his side holster, and let his hand rest lightly on the grip of his sidearm. "If you do not think I can clear this holster, and put a hole in your head before you get to me, it is only because you do not know me." He was a different animal now. The calm demeanor had given way to an ice cold killer instinct. He barely said a word after that; he would not even give me his name. "After the Commander talks to you, if he gives you the okay then we can talk."

We waited in silence for another ten minutes until I heard the rumble of vehicles headed our way. It appeared I was finally going to get my audience with the Commander, I just had to hope I could maintain my sanity long enough to make it to the research facility and show them exactly what they had done to us.

22

The man walking towards me was not what I expected at all. He was tall, and slender with graying hair, a salt and pepper beard, and was dressed in a plain black shirt, jeans, and tan work boots. When the young sniper had called him "Commander", followed by the entourage showing up in military vehicles, I was expecting a surly, battle scarred man in uniform. He looked almost stately, and had an easy smile.

I had moved out of the guard shack, and was standing at the curb in front with my shadow, who was still eyeing me suspiciously with his hand hanging near his pistol. The commander walked towards us, and my shadow stepped forward to meet him. "So what have we got here Jonathan?" The skinny sniper without a personality had a name after all.

Jonathan informed him of the situation briefly. His apathetic demeanor had returned, and he sounded bored out of his skull as he gave his report. The commander smiled, and thanked him for a job well done. With a hand shake, and a slap on the back he advanced past him, and made his way to me. He was accompanied by two men with guns, apparently his bodyguards, and others that stood in a haphazard circle around us. Most of them were as young as Jonathan, if not younger, and none of them looked the military type.

The bodyguard on the right was one of the few who looked older. He was probably early thirties like myself, with long dark hair pulled back into a ponytail, and, I'm not making this up, wore a sword on his back. He was an inch or two under six foot, Caucasian, with a large nose, pointed features, and eyes full of suspicion.

The other was shorter and stockier with shaggy hair, an awkward smile, and glasses. He looked like he should be playing video games not guarding a commander, but he was the only one I saw with a pistol on each hip, and not carrying a rifle. This was quite an odd crew.

The commander held out his hand as he approached, and I shook it.

"You guys go up the chain of command pretty fast here. I didn't think I would rate a commander right off the bat."

"Unfortunately our chain has been shortened dramatically on account of so many of the links dying. This is no longer a military base, just another place filled with survivors. Some are remnants of the military, others just residents from nearby towns, or travelers looking for safety. We're all just folk now. Besides, I have a standing order to be called when someone shows up who has heard the Call. But enough about us Isaac, let's talk about you, and your business at the lab."

"I'm just passing through, let me go to the lab, and then you will never have to deal with me again."

"So that means you either intend on staying for a prolonged amount of time, or you don't expect to live for much longer. How long since you heard the Call?"

"That's none of your business, let me through." My hands began to tremble again. My words came out deliberate, and strained. I could feel my body tensing. I was becoming increasingly frustrated with their failure to understand. I needed to get through, and I needed to do it right away. Frustration was giving way to desperation, and I was fighting to restrain my anger.

"Now hold on there. You don't have to go working yourself up like that. You couldn't fight your way through Jonathan; you can't do it against the whole team. Besides, your business isn't as urgent as you think."

"What?"

"You're obviously afraid that you're going to turn before you reach your destination, but you have more time than you think you do."

"How could you possibly know that for certain? No one knows that."

"The time between the Call and the turning often fluctuate, but the stages hardly ever do."

"What do you mean the stages never fluctuate?"

"The stages are pretty well known, but there are stages not everyone has noticed. Every stage has to happen before you turn, so if you're familiar with all of them, you can better predict the turning." He could see he had my complete attention at this point and continued. "For instance, if I were to shoot you in the leg right now it would hurt, but it would also heal almost instantly."

"Ya, Jonathan was nice enough to give me a demonstration earlier." Jonathan let a little half smile escape when I said this, and then quickly regained his mask of indifference. "I thought you were going to tell me something new."

"You may notice that your strength and speed are not quite as automatic." My silence and I am sure the look on my face, were enough to tell him what he needed to know. "I see, so you haven't made the connection yet. Healing is pretty automatic; if you get hurt your body recognizes the injury, and begins repairs. In your case these repairs happen instantly.

"Strength and speed work differently, they are more conscious actions. In the first stage you have to get worked up to increase your physical abilities. In the later stages it becomes as automatic as breathing. You have not reached that stage yet, so you still have some time."

"How much time do I have roughly?"

"Honestly, no clue. We still don't know why the times vary. We have some theories that we would like to try with you, if you don't object."

This caught me off guard. "What are you talking about? I don't have time for theories. I told you I am just passing through. "

"I'm sorry; I got a little ahead of myself there. Since you haven't advanced to the final stages yet I believe you still have time before you turn, perhaps a week or more. With our techniques I believe we can extend that time to three weeks, or maybe even a full month. I would like you to stay with us, and allow us to test these techniques on you. After that we will escort you to the facility."

"After that could be too late."

"I guess that all depends on the nature of your business there. What is the nature of your business there?"

"None of yours. That is its nature."

"Then I'm afraid I can't help you, and will have to ask you to leave."

This was not going well. I was not sure what this guy's angle was, or why he was so interested in me trying his "techniques", but I could not get by them so I was going to have to play his game. "Revenge is my business there. What exactly do you want from me?

"Interesting; that is a pretty vague answer but fair enough. If it's revenge you're after then I can't imagine you'll need much time for that. You play along with us, and I promise we'll get you into that facility with plenty of time to make whoever pay for whatever. As for what I want from you, well that part is fairly simple. The payment for passing through our base is all your supplies, and one hundred Haunted."

That was a price I was not expecting and I think my face displayed that fact pretty plainly. "You can't be serious. You're worse than the biker gangs back in Los Angeles!"

His tone and demeanor changed. He went from a calm, easy going manner to a colder more focused tone that had a dangerous edge to it. "Do not ever compare us to them. They take advantage of the situation of others for their own gain. We provide for everybody on this installation, both food and security. You don't have to pass through here, but if you do you are going to do your part. Usually the price of admission is fifty Haunted, but with your increased abilities one hundred should be a simple task. While you are with us you will be provided food and weapons, so you will not need yours. That is how it works; you can take it or leave it but do not ever compare us to those lowlifes again. They steal from people just trying to survive. We provide for people like that. If we steal it's only from thieves like them."

"So that makes you what, the Robin Hood of the apocalypse?"

He laughed loudly and returned to his former easy manner. "That is right son, and these are my merry men." The others all joined in the laughter at this. "And guess what? You just wandered into Sherwood forest, so if you want to pass you have to pay the toll."

"You really expect me to go out, find, and kill one hundred Haunted just to enter into your little club here?"

"Well not in one night! I'm not that crazy. Consider this a loan. We welcome you into our little community, and provide you food and shelter. We will also train you to kill the Haunted more proficiently, and in return you will put the skills we give you to good use, and get one hundred confirmed Haunted kills."

"You really think I need training? I just took them on two at a time with a knife. I'd think I've proven my skills."

"Let me explain something to you Isaac. Some groups fortify areas with good supplies and try to survive by holing up and waiting this thing out. Others go around gathering supplies and survivors, and stay on the run surviving by avoiding the Haunted and only fighting when needed for defense.

"We, on the other hand, believe that the best defense is a good offense. We do not scurry through the city trying to scrounge up supplies. We go there to hunt. We track these things down and take them out one by one, and we will keep doing this until this entire area is clear. Each man here has already paid his debt many times over, and this makes them the most experienced Haunted killing unit you are likely to find. They may look young, but every last one of them has forgotten more about killing these things than you have learned. They can teach you how to kill these things by the dozen, not just two at a time. If you want to learn then you can sign up. It will cost you exactly one hundred Haunted and all your supplies."

It was obvious at this point I was not getting through any other way. I had come this far, and I couldn't stop now. I had to take the chance. "Okay, sign me up Commander Hood."

"That would be Commander Allen actually, but do me a favor, and just call me Mark. Ranks don't really matter that much anymore."

Thomas Harwick

23

The supplies, guns, and ammo were quickly removed from my truck, and added to the arsenal of one of the military Hummers. They even took the weapons I was carrying, and told me I would be issued new ones when we got to the base. It took about ten minutes to drive from the South Gate to the actual base. The scenery was the same delightful combination of desolation, dirt, and weeds that I had been seeing ever since Palmdale.

When we got into the residential areas however, there was green grass and towering pine trees. We passed by a beautiful park and even a golf course. The green grass was splotched with yellowed patches here and there that would only get worse when summer came back around, but considering what I had been looking at for most of my trip it was pretty impressive.

On the way to my new home I was in the front seat of the Humvee that Mark was driving. We talked a little bit, but most of it was filled with my questions. Not that I got many useful answers.

When we finally arrived at our destination we pulled in front of what used to be a middle school. It was across the street from a section of housing, and Mark caught my inquisitive look.

"The school is our training area. We are going to start your training immediately, since you are in such a hurry. After a couple hours we'll eat, and call it a night. We can finish your training tomorrow, and go from there."

We got out of the Humvee, and the two bodyguards got out of the back seat. The Guard with the pony tail and sword stayed by Mark, while the shorter kid with shaggy hair and glasses stood next to me. "I have some other business to attend to so I leave you in Mason's capable hands."

Mason stuck his hand out sharply and shook mine quickly. He gave a little half smile and half muttered –half spoke "Well, let's get started." He suddenly turned away and began walking to the School. He was a twitchy little guy, and not much of a talker. He barely uttered a paragraph the whole time we trained.

Inside the school's gym was a pretty impressive training area, but we kept walking and went out the back door. We still had a couple hours before we lost the light, so we worked at the outside shooting range they had set up. It was basically just a wooden frame with a rail running across about four feet off the ground, and one running along the top four feet above that. There was an open expanse of grass in front of it and targets set up at several different distances.

The targets were mannequins barrowed from the Base Exchange clothing department. They were pretty destroyed and I didn't know how we were going to tell which bullet holes were mine until Mason walked over to a pile of pillow cases lying on the ground. He picked one up and placed it over the mannequin's head.

Someone had painted the pillow case with what was supposed to be a Haunted face. It looked more like a third grader drawing the boogeyman. It had two red eyes, complete with angry eyebrows, and cartoonish fangs with blood dripping off of them.

"We'll start with the up close and personal shot." Mason said as he moved the mannequin only about fifteen feet from where I was at. I started to protest that I already knew how to shoot, but he pretended not to hear me. "Just take your time and put two shots in its head if you can."

I decided to stop arguing and just get it over with. "Fine, whatever you say instructor." There may have been a hint of sarcasm in my voice there, but it did seem like a huge waste of time.

"Start whenever you are ready."

I lifted the Glock they had given me, took my aim and put one right in the middle of the pillow case. I was lining the second shot up still when something hit my hand and forced my arms off to the side as I squeezed the trigger. The shot sailed off into the distance and I was not sure what had happened at first.

I don't know why I didn't notice it before then, but there was a rope that was anchored from the middle of the top of the frame and ran down the side of the contraption. It had a sandbag weighting down the end of it about a foot off the ground and when Mason threw the sand bag my way it had turned the whole thing into a sort of homemade pendulum.

"What was that!?"

"Training" He answered like it was so obvious an answer that he was surprised by the question. "Do you really think that the Haunted are going to let you set up, and take aim like that? That target is fifteen feet away, which means that if it was a Haunted it would be on you in a single jump. That is how long you have to put two bullets right in its head."

I was frustrated, but I got set to try again anyway. I got two shots off, and got the gun down before the rope came swinging by, but the shots hit in the chest. "Anything that is not a kill point on the head is a miss, try again." I tried a few more times, my frustration growing with each try.

"Do you mind if I show you how it is done." The voice did not belong to Mason, and came from behind me. I set my gun on the rail and turned towards the voice.

Mason sounded like he was slightly annoyed when he answered. "Do you mind Nick? I am training the new guy."

"Well I just thought the noob would like to see a demonstration on how to do that drill properly." Nick was only slightly taller than Mason, and slightly thinner as well. He had blonde hair that was not quite as shaggy as Mason's, and was wearing an impish grin. He looked to be around eighteen or nineteen, but definitely no older than twenty.

Behind Nick was a much larger man. He stood about six feet tall, and had to be somewhere near to three hundred pounds. His size was only accented by his unkempt red beard that in no way matched his light brown hair except that it was also unkempt. He wore thick glasses, and had squinty eyes set into a face with rounded features.

He spoke with a voice that was not high, but also was not quite what I was expecting from a man his size. "I am sure he would love a demonstration from someone who knows what they're doing. I am just wondering what that has to do with you."

"What are you talking about? I am getting super fast at this."

"But you haven't hit one headshot, and we were out here for like three hours before we took that break."

"Well ya, but I was getting a lot closer at the end. I just need to get more shots off, one of them is bound to hit."

"Or you might try this new technique I heard about called aiming. It is all the rage right now." Mason piped in as the big guy shook with laughter.

"Why don't you try a technique called shutting your mouth" Nick replied angrily.

This went on for a few more minutes, and many more insults, until the big guy was practically rolling.

I was grateful for the amusement, since it took my mind off my frustrating training. I interrupted the argument, and handed my gun to Nick. "I need a break anyway; I would love to see how this is supposed to be done if you don't mind showing me."

He was positively glowing at this point. "No problem man, check this out." He accepted my firearm, and then surprised me by producing another one. He walked up to the rail, and said with an air of confidence "Alright, let's do this." Mason rolled his eyes and got into position at the rope. The big guy walked over to the other side where a second rope was attached, which got Nick's attention. "Tom, what are you doing?"

"You are using two guns, so you get two ropes. I mean, it only seems fair. Go ahead Nick; show us all how it is done.

This only strengthened Nick's resolve, and you could see the intense focus on his face. His grip on the twin guns tightened slightly, and the muscles in his arms and neck tensed up just a little. He was determined to prove them wrong. "At least get the ropes going first." Tom and Mason looked at each other, and agreed that it seemed fair enough, and set the ropes in motion.

Mason got his going first followed by Tom's. Nick let the ropes go by a couple times, following them with his eyes, and getting the timing down. When he was satisfied that he had it he stepped up and began firing.

I hate to admit it, but he was much more graceful than I was. He alternated the guns, first raising his right arm and squeezing three shots off, then in one motion swinging the right arm down while bringing his left arm up, and squeezing three shots off with that gun. He repeated this until he had fired nine shots from each gun.

With only one round left per gun he waited for the right moment, brought the two guns up together, fired simultaneously, and brought them back down just as one of the ropes swung by. He stood there with a big smile on his face. There was no doubt the kid was fast.

"Did you guys see that?" He could barely contain his own excitement.

Tom was the first to respond. "We did, very pretty. Mason, how many Haunted did he kill?

"Not a single one."

"So you got torn to shreds by the Haunted without taking a single one with you, but at least you looked good doing it right?"

Nick was quiet and sullen. The rest of us couldn't contain our laughter. His face grew serious as he began reloading both guns. Tom regained his composure first, and questioned Nick's actions. "Nick, what are you doing?"

"I am going to get this down."

"Seriously? I have to go start making dinner for everybody and I need your help."

"I am not leaving until I get this." He was resolute and Tom apparently saw there was no arguing this point, because he threw his hands up in resignation, and then walked to the rope to get it into position. Nick took three more turns much to the chagrin of Tom and Mason.

After turn three Tom tried to take him to the side and advise him. "You keep trying to take three or four shots at a time, but you only need one good shot. You should concentrate on taking that one good shot, and then worry about following it up with others later. It also might be a little easier with one gun. Duel wielding is awesome in video games, but clumsy and difficult in reality."

"I get what you're saying, but I am not that great of a shot and more bullets give me a better chance of success. I mean, it's just basic math."

"You were shooting before you even got your arm raised all the way! I swear you almost put a couple into the rail for crying out loud." His tone betrayed his exasperation and hinted that this was not the first time they had debated this way. It went back and forth like this for a while. At one point Mason tried to explain it to him too, but it had no effect.

Finally Tom apparently had reached his breaking point. "Fine I tell you what, you let Mason show you how it is supposed to be done, and then we will figure out how to do it your way. Stay here, I'll be right back."

"Where are you going?"

"If it's more bullets you want, then I will get you more bullets." And with that he walked in the back of the gym and disappeared.

Mason switched places with Nick and I moved to the other rope. He had one gun in his side holster and one in his hands. He got into a comfortable shooting stance and focused in on the target. He looked completely different when he was preparing to shoot. He kept his gun down below the rail as he spoke to us. His voice was no longer a mumble, but with the clear authoritative voice of a teacher.

"You still have to take your time and aim, you just have to do it faster. Focus only on hitting that target, and when you see a shadow in your peripheral bring the gun down.

That is the easiest way. After you start to hit your target it is just a matter of repetition until it becomes ingrained in your muscles themselves. After you do it enough you arm will just jump back to where it was almost automatically. Go ahead and start the ropes."

Nick threw his first, followed by mine. We timed it so that there was maybe a second and a half between ropes. Mason let both go by, but as soon as the second one had cleared he had the gun up, and took his time taking aim. It was less than two seconds, but it seemed longer. He took careful aim and did not seem rushed at all when the rope came into his periphery. He squeezed the trigger and got the gun down just as the rope flew by. The following shots were much faster.

He was right; as soon as he drew his bead it seemed like he could drop his arm, and bring it immediately back to the exact same spot. Rope, bang! Rope, bang! It continued this way until he emptied the first gun. As he brought his arm down he let the empty gun fall and pulled the gun from his side holster in a single move. With the second gun he fired twice for each pass. Rope, bang! Bang! Rope, bang! Bang! I was starting to believe what Commander Allen had said about these guys being the best of the best for killing Haunted. If all of them were this good he was probably right. Probably.

When Mason was done he picked up the gun he had dropped. "It is not the best way to treat your gun, but I wanted to make a point. When you are out there, and you have multiple Haunted coming at you, sometimes you won't have time to holster your weapon. Empty it, drop it, and replace it. That is the only way you will be making it out alive."

"He is pretty good right?" The voice was behind us and I recognized it as Tom's. He was back and he had two mini Uzis in his hands. "If you want a lot of bullets in a little time then these ought to do the trick."

"Where did you get these?"

"That is kind of a long story. Suffice it to say that I had a bit of a run in with some gang members a while back and they do not need them anymore so they are all yours."

Nick had a big goofy grin about a mile wide as he accepted the twin bullet hoses. "It's like Christmas day as a kid, but way better."

Tom chuckled. "Just go shoot the stupid things so we can cook some dinner will you?"

Mason put a fresh pillow case on the target with a new and interesting face, and Nick tried again with his new weaponry. He had the same flashy technique as before and the same terrible accuracy as well. This time however, the bullets started near the bottom of the mannequin, and trailed upward, ending with a couple shots in the face and head. When he finished he took a moment to enjoy his handiwork.

Mason made his way over to look at the pillow case and after a few seconds called out. "Well most of them missed the head miserably. A few of them are superficial, and would not do much more than mess up his looks, but there are at least three kill shots here."

Nick let out a triumphant fist pump and Tom quickly said "Works for me, let's go cook up some grub."

I stayed at the makeshift range with Mason for another hour or so before he left to go eat. I told him I wanted some more practice and he laughed and told me not to waste all the bullets. As I recall they had to send Commander Allen himself to drag me back for dinner after another hour or so. After watching Mason I knew I needed to master that technique as soon as possible, and by the end of the night I was getting pretty close.

24

The flames of the fire leapt high, and engulfed the large pan that was holding our food. Making it hiss, and sizzle, and pop in a tantalizing combination of the sight of the flames, and the smells and sounds of the food. The aroma crept through the crisp night air, and settled in around us. The temperature had plummeted a good thirty degrees after the sun made its retreat for the day, which is not uncommon in the Mojave Desert. The cold wind rushed in from off of the Sierra Mountain Range with nothing to stand against the onslaught but the tumble weeds. The sky was cloudless and bright with stars, and between it and the fire, our little gathering was very well lit.

These meals were an event unto themselves. Fresh foods were very rare, and most of our meals came from a can, but Tom and Nick did everything they could to dress them up as gourmet feasts. I believe that first meal was ramen fried up with soy sauce, and spam, and every spice imaginable thrown in. It might not sound like cuisine, but huddled around that fire, and smelling those aromas wafting through the cold night air, I can say without a doubt that was one of the finest meals I have ever enjoyed.

The herbs and spices came from a pretty extensive little garden Tom's father had kept. Tom and Nick had been tending it ever since he died. They did not offer any more details than that and I did not pry. One of the most galvanizing things about our new world is that everyone has lost someone. Nick was Tom's nephew, and though they seemed to fight on pretty much every issue, food was something they could usually agree on.

That first dinner was quite interesting. Being forced to be there I was not overly social; however, I found that with this group that was not much of a problem. They set out right away to make me feel more at ease. The rest of the night was spent in noisy, spirited conversation, and included many stories about the base and the people in it. It was a lot to take in, and many of the stories were exaggerated, but I was able to glean many tidbits of information, and piece together a working knowledge about the group I was now in.

Considering how much I stress that my time is limited, it may seem odd that I would devote so much time to my first day of training, and that first dinner. The simple fact is that I spent three weeks and some change with them, and in that short amount of time I became very close to several of the members. I will only have time to recount for you a few stories and select missions. You will not have the time to learn about these men that I had, but it is important to me that you get to know them as much as is possible through mere words on paper.

Mark was with us for that first meal, and most of the first week. But in his role as Commander he had to make the rounds from team to team, and was not always able to dine with us. I learned that the base had many more people on it than I had thought originally. They split up the housing areas, and the duties into teams. Those who could not fight were put to work in other ways, cooking, cleaning, whatever they were able to contribute. Those who could fight were split into teams, and provided the security for the base. They rotated the teams to different areas, and schedules, and everything was done quite professionally, and efficiently.

The team I was on was different though. It was the only team allowed on search and destroy missions. The other teams might be sent out to gather supplies on occasion, but ours was the only team dedicated solely to killing the Haunted, and the members took great pride in that. They had emerged as an elite squad of sorts, and were as odd in their behavior as they were proficient in their killing. All in all Mark always seemed particularly proud of this motley crew of his.

I confirmed my suspicions that Mark was military prior to the Haunted, but I never learned how high up the food chain he had risen. I know that he was not the Commander of the base when the outbreak first happened, but had assumed command when the acting Commander turned. That was the extent of the information that I was able to glean from him though. It was during our conversation that he introduced me to his rule about never mentioning the past. As a result, I can't give you very many details about his or any other member of the team's history.

Another interesting fact I learned was that there was still electricity to the Base, to a degree. This was not the case for much of the quarantine zone. Not many employees were willing to stick around to maintain and monitor the electrical grids, and the Haunted were very destructive. I doubt it was their plan to black out our power, but it was one of the results of their devastation. As such, finding areas with working electricity was rare, and this base was one of them. The lab that I was heading to, as well as several more necessary buildings were kept running through a combination of backup generators, and solar power.

This particular base had rows of solar panels in a sort of energy farm that collected and distributed it to the buildings that the Military deemed "mission essential." Some of the housing was even hooked up to these systems, although this squad never used them. Mike, the pony tailed guy with the sword, told me later that "it just wouldn't be a proper apocalypse if we weren't roughing it." Like I said, they were an odd crew.

The next revelation was the most interesting yet however, as I learned that there existed some small measure of cooperation between the medical research facility, and Commander Allen's team. The cooperation was slight, and the alliance shaky, but the two groups realized that they could benefit each other. Mark's group provided a sort of buffer between the researchers, and the Haunted. Their control of the Base also insured there would be little chance of gangs, or desperate survivors making any kind of attempt to raid the Laboratory.

For the part of the researchers they were useful in a couple of ways. For one, they were the ones maintaining the solar panels. Besides just medical researchers they had expert technicians keeping the power to the research facility up. As part of the agreement they left the power to mission essential buildings alone, and were actually the ones who hooked some of the housing, and the training building into the system.

One of the things that had turned public opinion away from the researchers was the fact that though the entire area had been quarantined, and communications blocked to "prevent mass hysteria", the researchers seemed to have a direct line out. It made sense to some degree. They were supposedly still working on a cure, and couldn't leave the facility, but would need to replenish their medical supplies as well as food and weaponry. That did not keep most people from resenting them when supplies were air lifted in by helicopter.

Though most people resented them for their connections to the outside world, Mark's group used this to their benefit. By the time Mark had taken command most of the military personnel on the Base was either dead, or had been sent as support in L.A., and therefore also dead. This caused him to adopt a more open philosophy on enlistment. This meant that he no longer had personnel that were trained on things like the radar system.

The Military would not risk losing anyone else to the mysterious virus so reinforcements were out of the question. Mark was more or less told that they were on their own and his last orders were to make the best stand they could, and take as many Haunted with them as possible. Mark convinced the researchers to use their connections in the corporation to find someone willing to at least try to train Mark's people on running the Base's radar system. This was the second way the researchers proved useful. Luckily, Mark happened to have a tech savant on his team who was able to learn the system.

His tech genius was tall and gangly, with bright red hair, freckles, and glasses that were so thick they were practically telescopic. His name was Matt, he was Jonathan's older brother, and apparently he was to technology as Jonathan was to long range shooting.

He actually joined us for that dinner, and several after. I became pretty familiar with his role on the team. Matt was as outgoing and talkative as his younger brother was quiet. In accordance with Mark's rule he gave no specific details about his past except to say that he had always had a "talent" with technology.

It wasn't just that he was good using computers either; he had quite the knack for building them as well. He was nearly blind, and useless for most jobs, but he was invaluable as the team's resident computer geek. He had managed to teach the basics of the radar to a handpicked team of techies affectionately known as the nerd horde.

This allowed us to borrow him from time to time for missions where we needed eyes and ears on the streets. He had the ability to hack camera systems much like the researchers had been doing to study us, and came in handy in other various geek ways.

I helped myself to seconds while Matt went on excitedly about the radar. The steam poured from the noodles, snaking its way through the night air as Matt talked on and on about the wonders of their system. Supposedly it could track anything larger than a coyote in a twenty mile radius, but I never confirmed this because I just didn't care enough. If it was true, then it only confirmed that joining the group, and paying my dues was the only way I was going to get near that facility.

When we were full of warm food, and quite content by the fire, the stories shifted to the events from earlier that day. Jonathan recounted my arrival in his usual lazy manner, and offered a half hearted apology for shooting me in the kneecap. I waved it off, saying I had given him no choice. It turned out that it was just by chance he was there at all. An incident that was never fully explained to me had caused them to be short handed at that gate, and Jonathan had volunteered his services leading to our eventful meeting.

Mason took over the conversation at this point, and described in great comedic detail, the exchange of words between Commander Allen and myself. When he got to the part where I compared Mark to Robin Hood the rest of the group exploded into laughter, and after they heard his response they decided to adopt the moniker "The Merry Men". During my time there they would go so far as to spray paint "The Merry Men were here" and "Merry Men Fight Back" on multiple surfaces throughout the cities we hunted in.

The stories and revelry continued well into the night in the same boisterous manner. They started speaking in an odd mix of inside jokes, and videogame jargon that might as well have been a different language. Mark was silent for most of the meal. Occasionally he would interject with a humorous remark or anecdote, but mostly he just sat there half smiling, taking it all in.

Well into the night he got to his feet, let out a large yawn, and addressed us. "Well gentlemen, I think it's about time for this old geezer to call it a night." Turning to me "you might want to get some sleep too if you can. The fun will be starting dark and early tomorrow."

25

My training consisted of two programs – combat, and control. In combat training I practiced shooting with Mason, and melee combat with Mike. The second program was focused more on control. Teaching me to harness and control my enhanced abilities without having to enter a state of rage, and also attempting to control the speed of my conversion. The control program could be broken down into medical and mental, but I will get into those a little later.

Combat training took up most of that first day, and did indeed start quite early. Firearms training with Mason went much the same as the day before. He had some other unorthodox drills, and alternate shooting positions to use when the Haunted got too close. It all boiled down to learning to get the gun up, aimed, and firing as fast and accurate as possible.

We also discussed some of the basic tactics we would be using in the upcoming missions to track them down, flush them out, and take them down. I was already markedly better than the previous day, and continued to advance as the day wore on. In the late afternoon I moved on to my training with Mike.

Mike was crazy. That is not my opinion, but just plain point of fact. I'm not saying it wasn't justified, but simply that it is what he was. I've said before that the common denominator between all of us was the loss of loved ones. Mike was no exception, and had one of the more heartbreaking stories in the group. But that did not change that he was completely, and utterly nuts.

Most conversations with him consisted of either random quotes from Sun Tzu's "Art of War", or ridiculous statements that were probably meant to be jokes, at least I hope so. Other times he would spout on about the "True way of the warrior". These habits, along with his affinity for fighting the Haunted with nothing but a Samurai Sword, earned him the nickname "Samurai Mike."

I learned later, and mostly from the others, that Mike had a wife and three children when the Haunted outbreak began. I have nothing but empathy for him after having to watch my own wife as this "disease" tore at her sanity. He wasn't able to kill his wife, and so she completed the transformation, overpowered him, and killed their three children. A large part of him broke that day, and will never be fixed. He managed to kill her then, and keep his children from turning. From that point on his mission was to kill as many Haunted as possible before he dies, which made him a perfect fit for Mark's group.

I think he does it to free those who have turned, or maybe so that their loved ones don't have to. Either way it is his mission, and he carries it out without any perceivable emotion. He prefers to fight up close, like a true warrior, and so he favors a sword. "Swords don't need to be reloaded" is the reasoning he usually gives. I think killing those monsters is all that's left for him until he dies. Like me he won't commit suicide, but I am pretty sure he means to fall in battle.

Even before my experiences with the Haunted I was no stranger to fighting, but this was something else all together.

Mike had developed his own fighting style based solely on the Haunted, and the way they move. "Know thy self, know thy enemy. A thousand battles, a thousand victories." The Haunted are hyper aggressive, and sadistic, and as such they become very predictable. They charge forward, tend to go for the throat, and like to savor the kill.

Knowing their movements is the key; however, their lightning speed makes them hard to hit even when you know how they will attack you. You have to learn them to the point of predicting them, reacting even before they begin to move. "Now the reason the enlightened prince and the wise general conquer the enemy whenever they move, and their achievements surpass those of ordinary men, is foreknowledge."

The next thing his style combats is their incredible strength. After you predict the attack you have to move with it, using the strength and momentum of the Haunted against itself. You have to provide yourself as an easy target and then at the last opportunity remove that target, and counter the attack. "All war is deception. Be extremely subtle, even to the point of formlessness. Be extremely mysterious, even to the point of soundlessness. Thereby you can be the director of the opponent's fate."

Every attack was purposeful and meant to kill or disable. They focused on the only areas that seemed vulnerable on a Haunted, the head and the legs. The head is a target for obvious reasons, and the legs because even a Haunted can't stand without a base. The defense seemed at times to almost be a dance, but when the opening showed itself the attacks were lightning quick, and without any frivolous or wasted movements. "Invincibility lies in the defense, and the possibility of victory in the attack."

We covered a lot of hand to hand combat, but we also went over blade techniques as well. That first day was mostly just him spouting sayings, and explaining his fighting style, but after he had run me through some of the more basic maneuvers we sparred for an hour before calling it a day.

He had a much different view on sparring than most, so I should probably elaborate. Before starting he told me that if my goal was to learn how to control my abilities and how to kill Haunted than I should continue. If I was not willing to kill or be killed, to sell out to his method no matter the cost that I should turn back. I told him that everything in me had already died, and I only had my purpose left. He asked me what my purpose was, and when I answered with a single word he smiled.

"Vengeance? That is a good answer." He reached his right hand slowly up to his left shoulder as he spoke. Strapped to the shoulder were four throwing knives, he drew two of them, and held one in each hand. "It seems that I have finally met a kindred soul. If you mean that then attack me, and hold nothing back. Draw your knife and put everything into it. Your hate, anger, fear, regret, you will need all of it. Put everything you are and everything you have been through into that blade, and then give it to me if you can"

I hesitated at first, it all seemed so crazy, but somehow I knew that this had to be done. I pulled my knife and struck at him. The first few attacks were half hearted, and he easily batted them aside. On my third try I lunged towards him, and brought the knife straight at him in a stabbing motion. He was right in front of the blade and then he just wasn't.

I think his body had begun the quick spin move before my blade even started towards him. He simply spun around my strike and moved along my arm bringing his blade up under my arm and into my stomach with explosive force. Blood spilled everywhere as I fell backwards in pain, my strength draining.

He looked down at me and smiled. "You'll live. This time please take me seriously. I don't like wasting my time."

By the time I struggled back up to my feet my wound was already healed, and my strength was returning. My teeth were clenched, and I was breathing heavily. I could feel the anger rising as I struck out again.

My strikes were faster, my intentions far more serious, and yet the results were much the same. He would slip by my strikes and give me a cut, usually on the arms, slowly covering the ground in my blood.

"You could at least give me your best effort. I am rolling out the red carpet for you after all." He smiled as he dodged another blow and added to the "carpet" he was making. He continued to taunt me as I lumbered about slipping and sliding in my own blood. The anger and frustration built rapidly as I kept swinging in futility until I ran headlong into a wall of rage.

My speed instantly doubled and the quick change nearly caught him, but at the last instant he let himself collapse to the ground, falling under my attack, and landing on his side just in front of my legs. He brought his knife around to the back of my right foot and cut my Achilles tendon, then brought the handle hard into the back of my knee forcing me to fall forward over him.

As I fell forward he rolled the opposite way and got back to his feet. I picked myself up, hobbling at first until my tendon healed, turned back towards him full of nothing but the bloodlust of a Haunted.

The rest of my recollections of the fight are a little blurry; I had lost control and was fighting him as a Haunted. I do remember him smiling as he got into his stance. We were finally getting down to business, and this was exactly what he wanted. I let out an inhuman scream, and charged straight at him, just like any Haunted, and released an unrelenting flurry of powerful strikes.

He was an illusion. I would have had an easier time fighting a mirage. He slipped past my attacks like water through my fingers. I remember that it never seemed like he was moving that fast, just that every attack seemed to miss him. He used the absolute minimum movement required to dodge each blow, and always seemed to start that movement before the attack took place.

This went on seemingly forever, which in this case was about ten minutes, until Mike began trying to calm me down. He had stopped antagonizing me with cuts, and had dropped his knife altogether. Slowly I fought back into control of myself, falling to my knees, and shaking as I forced myself to calm down. It took several minutes this time.

Mike walked up to me and placed a hand on my shoulders as he crouched down beside me. "That was very good for our first try. Every day we will manipulate you into your Haunted state, and then pull you back out. I want you to try as hard as you can to think strategically while you are in that mode. We need to channel your rage into purpose. You will never hit me in the state you were just in, stampeding around with all the subtlety of a rhino. Your goal is to force yourself into strategic movement while still enraged enough to stay in your Haunted mode."

I guess I should have told you that Mike was also my teacher for the mental part of my training. We trained almost nonstop for three days before my first mission. Three days may not seem like an ample amount of training time, but time was not exactly on our side so it would have to do. That doesn't mean the training stopped there though.

Most of our missions took place in the late afternoon. We didn't want to stay out too late and hunt in the dark, but we tried to wait until after the hottest part of the day. That left the early mornings and into the afternoon for training. It was not a schedule that allowed for much beauty sleep, but I wasn't sleeping much at this point anyway.

After Mike was done using me as a pin cushion Mark showed up to chauffer me himself to the medical facility where I was poked, and prodded some more. The clinic was one of the select buildings that still had power, and as we approached it I couldn't help but be a little wary of our purpose.

This was nothing like the researchers and their facilities however. There weren't scores of Doctors and scientists waiting to dissect me, but only a skeleton crew of people with basic medical knowledge, and not a Doctor among them. They weren't attempting to develop some miracle treatment; they just wanted to run a few simple tests.

They made some observations, and drew some blood. They said they'd run some tests then get back to me, and sent me on my way to the final stop.

We swung by the camp first so that I could change into some clothes that were a little less blood soaked. It was dark by this time, but our destination was one of the houses that had been wired into the solar power. It was a small one story house with yellowing stucco walls, and a basketball hoop out front. There looked to have been a lawn once, but now it was just a yellow patch of dried grass that crunched under our feet. There was a garage off to the right, and latticework filled with the dried remains of some kind of vine running along the side of it.

Mark opened the door and ushered me into a crème colored room containing a pair of dark brown couches, and a fully stocked bookshelf. Between the two couches was an overstuffed chair of the same deep brown. The chair was occupied by a small man who looked comical sitting in the large chair. Almost as if the overstuffed piece of furniture was preparing to swallow him whole. Mark smiled and said "Isaac, I'd like you meet the Chappy."

The small man in the large chair immediately hopped up, and made his way over to me with pep in his step. He was only an inch or two over five feet tall, thin, with shaggy blonde hair lazily flipped to one side. He wore black framed glasses, and a genuine smile that were both too big for his face. He shook my hand with more vigor than I was prepared for.

He spoke in an excited voice that was not exactly high pitched, but it sure wasn't a bass, with just a bit of a nasal sound to it. "Good to meetcha, good to meetcha. Come on in, and make yourself right at home. My name is Jeremy, but you can call me chaplain or chappy if you like. Whatever you are comfortable with. Go ahead and sit down if you want, and we can get started. First of all, welcome to the Chapel."

That is pretty much how Chappy was the whole time just talking away at a mile a minute. He was an excitable little guy, and I pretty much liked him instantly. He was wearing a shirt for a sports team that happened to be the rival of the team my wife and I used to root for, so much of our initial conversation was good natured banter about the rivalry.

It's not that either of us really cared about something that trivial anymore, but sometimes it is nice to remind yourself there was a time when we could. Mark had departed chuckling during our conversation, and left me with the hyperactive Chaplain. After the small talk had been more or less exhausted, we got down to brass tacks and Chappy explained to me what I was doing here.

The explanation dragged on for a little while, so I will give you the summary here. The control portion of the training program could be broken down into medical, and mental. Mike was part of that mental process, but Chappy was the other half. Mike's training was meant to teach me control over my abilities, but Chappy's portion was focused on controlling my actual conversion into a Haunted, or at least slowing it down.

His plan basically boiled down to therapy of a sort. I seriously doubt that it has changed the time it has taken for me to be driven crazy, but it has made the trip slightly more enjoyable. His approach was mostly a variation of a technique from the Bible, "taking every thought into captivity".

For our experiment this basically just meant that I had to teach myself to stop and examine any thought that was especially angry or vengeful, and get rid of it. It sounds overly simplistic, and it really is, but they were trying just about anything they thought might help even a little, and I was open to suggestions.

Chappy also gave me a small blue hardbound notebook and told me to write down my experiences from each day before I went to sleep. He laughed pretty hard when I asked him if I should begin each entry with "Dear Diary". He said that basically we were just trying to give me a way to keep my mind focused and rooted in reality and fend off the mad logic that would soon be creeping into my thinking. Every time that my nightmares kept me awake I was to record them in exact detail in my book. This technique actually has worked quite well and is part of the reason I am writing this current record.

After that we mostly just talked. Despite the fact that he was usually a twitchy ball of energy, he actually was a great listener. We would talk about my experiences, life on the base, his faith, the Bible, or sometimes we would just talk. I am not one for psychiatry, but that is not what this felt like. He had a different personality than Jacob, but the heart was the same. He just had that quality about him that put you at ease, and made people gravitate towards him no matter their beliefs.

As I got up to leave at the end of our session I hesitated slightly before turning to leave, and he picked up on it. "Did you have something else you wanted to talk about Isaac?"

"I wanted to ask you something, but I don't want to offend you by questioning your God."

He smiled warmly. "I have heard it said that faith is in the business of giving answers, and without questions it goes out of business. Simply put, God wants us to question Him, as long as we are willing to hear the answer."

"That sounds fair. That sounds like something my wife would have said actually. She always used to say that all things work to good if you love God, that He uses even the bad things for His purpose."

"That would be Romans eight twenty eight, slightly paraphrased of course."

I nodded my head slightly. "It was her favorite verse. My question would be.."

"What could possibly be the purpose for all of this? How could God use any of this for good?" I nodded again. "I get that question a lot. That is hard to answer because we don't think like God. We don't see this life the same way. Your question assumes that God is real, and has control over this world, but lets his people die anyway. That thinking has a flaw though, and is a little unfair."

"If the Bible is true and God is real, then Heaven is also real. If that is true then it becomes a matter of perspective. So often we ask God to act, to heal our loved ones, and when they die we ask why He didn't. If we really believe He is real though then isn't that exactly what happened? I know you don't want to hear clichéd sayings like she is in a better place, but just because it is cliché doesn't mean it is wrong."

"The other thing to keep in mind is that according to this new perspective the most important thing to God would be to get you into His presence in Heaven, no matter what He had to let happen to you on Earth to get you there."

"You think God would allow something this horrible just to get our attention?"

"Wouldn't you, if it was truly the only way to save the one you love?"

"It would be nice to know there was something good behind all this evil. I would really like to believe that, I just don't know if I can."

"You might be surprised what you can do when God finally gets a hold of you. Like I said, it is okay to question, just listen for the answer. It might take some time but He always answers."

I said goodnight and stepped into the icy embrace of the night air filled with more questions and doubts, but also a little more hope than when I had stepped in. Mark had left me with a talkie, and told me to radio in if I wanted a ride.

The Chapel was no more than a mile from the camp, so I walked. I used the walk through the crisp night to try and process everything that had been happening to me up to this point. At the camp I skipped dinner, went to my tent and collapsed in exhaustion.

26

The next day they brought two troop carrier trucks around to our camp. Mark picked fourteen of us, and told us to get ready for a trip into town. We got underway in the late afternoon, and by about five we were in Lancaster setting up our base of operations. We moved in teams of three through the surrounding area flushing the Haunted out of any buildings.

The area we chose for that first mission was a series of small shopping centers directly off the freeway very soon after entering the city. The routine seemed to be that we first find an elevated position to put our snipers in that would give them an unobstructed view of the entire target area. Jonathan of course was the primary sniper, and the second sniper spot was rotated between a few of the better marksman on the team. On that day it was Mason, who was probably the only other Merry Man that could shoot anywhere near Jonathan's level with a rifle.

The second step was to leave the vehicles at the beginning of the street with two drivers who would come extract us if things got too interesting. Step three required two three man teams to set up outside the buildings, as firing squads basically, while two other three man teams went inside to flush the Haunted out into the open.

I was teamed with the bickering duo of Tom and Nick, which had already made for an interesting car ride. Since Nick and I had yet to repay any of our debt we were given the job of flushing the Haunted from the buildings. Acting as the bait did let us have the first look at them, but engaging the Haunted in close quarters was not highly recommended. Most of our job was getting their attention and luring them outside to be gunned down by the other team.

As the day progressed in this manner I could see the frustration building in Nick. He became less talkative, and his responses were short but hardly sweet. A dark mood settled in about him like a fog that refused to lift. Our team's basic strategy was that Nick and I would lead with silenced pistols, and Tom would bring up the rear with his Auto shotgun if things got out of hand.

I wasn't sure when we started if having a guy who looked like an offensive lineman was wise when our job was to get chased out of buildings by Haunted. But Tom turned out to be quite skilled in close quarters with a shotgun, and got us out of some uncomfortable situations more than once that day. I had managed a few kills myself, but Nick had gone the whole day getting nothing but a growing sense of aggravation.

We cleared several shopping centers and made our way down to the end of the Avenue. The only two structures left were a movie theater, and across the street a minor league baseball stadium. These had to be tackled differently than our previous stops. These were buildings that housed large amounts of people and could very well have been used as refuge when things had gone south.

It was decided that we would leave the stadium alone on this trip. It was just off the freeway but sat much lower, so we had already gotten a look at the field, and had seen that it housed several hundred Haunted. So instead we set our sights on the theater.

The theater boasted twenty two screens housed in a large and rather plain looking square building. The front had been adorned with movie posters and several large pillars holding up an overhang that was crowded with lights, and sheltered the long abandoned ticket booths. The structure was topped by three of what looked like the smoke stacks from a large steamboat. They were painted bright red with black trim on top, and to this day I still don't quite know what to make of them.

Being surrounded by nothing except a parking lot and a large expanse of dirt the whole thing made for a pretty absurd sight. Now that the posters were sun worn and the lights had all gone out it was also an eerie one. Through the doors we could see movement around the concession area so there was probably a straggler or two in the main lobby.

With twenty two screens that meant there were twenty two enclosed rooms with an unknown number of Haunted behind each one. None of us liked that setup, so it was decided that one team would go in and clear the main lobby, one team would stay just outside the front doors for backup, and the remaining two teams would sweep the perimeter of the building, and surrounding area for any stray Haunted. Jonathan and Mason clambered on top of a large SUV in the parking lot that gave them a nice slightly elevated view through the doors, and into the lobby. The drivers parked up on the main road between the Theater and Stadium in case we needed an emergency extraction.

Everyone could tell Nick was about to explode if he didn't get a kill today, so our team was selected to go inside. We stepped cautiously through the glass doors and into a large open area. On our left was a small eating area and kitchen that had a sign above it announcing it in a flowing script as the "Hollywood Café."

To our right was an arcade with space themed décor. I think it was called the "Galactic Arcade" or something to that effect. Straight ahead was the snack bar in all its gold trimmed glory. Like most theaters it looked like it was trying to hearken back to the good ol' days of Grand playhouses, but succeeded only in conveying a deep love of the color gold, marble floors, and scrollwork on every conceivable surface.

We were losing daylight by the minute, and the amount of light allowed to stab through the front doors was slight to begin with. We had flashlights with us but were avoiding turning them on because the downside to having a bright light in a dark room is that any Haunted in that room will be attracted to it. The small fingers of light straining to reach into the room were enough for us to at least check the café and arcade. We moved first to the "Hollywood Café".

It was done with more of the classic coffee house look with liberal use of the color brown. The chairs were tall and painted to look like dark wood, instead of whatever cheaper wood they were actually made from. Cracked brown pleather covered the seat. The tables were similarly tall and painted, and were incredibly small circles. The counter was stainless steel with a glass case that once held overpriced pastries but which was now empty.

As we passed through I had to laugh when I glanced at the menu and saw one of the items was an "Al Cappuccino." We needed the lights for the kitchen, but it checked out empty so we made our way to the arcade.

It checked out also, and we began to make our way out, but not before Nick jokingly begged Tom for some quarters.

The big guy let out a laugh. "Nick we're hunting super powered zombies in a dimly lit movie theater, we pretty much live in a video game now. The only difference is there is no reset button in our version, so focus up." Even in the low light I could tell nick was rolling his eyes. After they were done with that exchange we set our sights on the snack bar.

As we were heading that way a shadow flew across our field of vision and landed with a crash behind the snack bar. Our guns went up, our steps became slow and deliberate, and we moved in unison as we advanced. We were spaced evenly with Tom and me taking the wings while Nick had the middle. As we got closer we could hear it make a guttural growling sound, and our breathing slowed as we peered over the counter.

We got caught off guard plain and simple. Instead of one Haunted ready to attack, we found two Haunted fighting.

A few mistakes were made in those next few seconds. The first was that Tom and I were slow to react to the situation. The second was that Nick was quick to react to the situation, and the third was that he alerted the Haunted to our presence. One was a large middle aged man with black hair and a thick salt and pepper beard. His hair had been ripped out in patches and his clothes were shredded.

He was pinning a much smaller Haunted who looked to be a teenager with shaggy brown hair and blood covering his clothes and hands. The larger one had the little one's arms pinned and was attempting to rip its throat out with its teeth. Nick couldn't help letting out his amazement "Holy crap look at that!" When he realized he had just alerted it to our presence he rushed to squeeze off a shot before taking proper aim.

The combination of the rushed shot and the Haunted bringing its head up at the noise caused the shot to go through the neck instead of the head, and there was no time for a second. By the time Tom and I started to move our guns to take aim it was already making its move. In one motion it backhanded the gun from Nick's grasp with its left arm while turning its body, planting its right hand on the counter and hoisting itself over.

It grabbed Nick by the throat and lifted him straight off the ground. Its back was to me but I couldn't risk a shot going through and hitting Nick. It was holding Nick in front of Tom to block his shot, and I knew that it would only be a matter of moments before it broke Nick's neck or strangled him to death.

I had to close the gap and try to get a better angle for a shot that wouldn't hit Nick in the process. Just as I was getting my muscles to respond to my brain's call to action I heard a booming sound like a small explosion. Blood and bits of tissue splashed across the floor in front of me, and the Haunted dropped Nick as it fell to the ground in a heap.

Tom had been quicker to react than me, and when the Haunted lifted Nick off the floor he immediately let the barrel to his shotgun fall, and took aim at the things foot. The move had taken away its base momentarily, and forced it to release Nick, but it was far from dead.

It struggled to gain enough traction on the blood slicked floor to leap at Tom. Its stump of a right leg was flailing about, but it got just enough push from its left foot to send itself falling into Tom before he could get a second shot off. It hit him with a sort of flailing shoulder tackle and they both tumbled to the ground.

The Haunted had gotten both hands on the shotgun, and was pushing it against Tom's throat to choke him to death.

Tom was a large and moderately strong man, but against a Haunted his throat should have been crushed instantly; however the things foot was still forming and it had not managed yet to get the leverage needed to use its full strength.

Again I found myself in a situation where taking the shot also meant risking the bullet going through and hitting a teammate. By this time however, Nick had managed to retrieve his weapon and roll himself up to one knee. This time Nick made sure he had the shot before squeezing the trigger, and for the second time in a matter of seconds my teammate saved me from an impossible decision.

Nick stayed kneeled with his gun outstretched for several seconds letting it all sink in. Slowly a smile began to crawl its way across his face until it reached nearly ear to ear. Nick had just got his first official Haunted kill, and he had saved his uncle's life in the process. It didn't matter that Tom had saved Nick's life just moments before. It would be a long time before he let his uncle live it down.

I went to help Tom back up while Nick began his celebration. I was chuckling as I extended my hand to help the big man up. He was shaking his head as he struggled back to his feet. "Well, there goes any chance of this being a stealth mission. You might think about toning down your victory dance Nick, or we're going to have every other..." His voice trailed off and his expression changed just as an alarming realization dawned in my mind.

"The other one!" It was both question and statement and Tom and I shouted it practically in unison. The larger Haunted had pinned and ripped out the throat of a smaller Haunted, but that was not a mortal wound to them. The bigger Haunted had not killed it, and we had not shot it, so where was it?

Nick's celebration had carried him back over towards the counter, and he was standing with his back turned to it when the meaning of our exclamation hit him. He tried to swing to face the counter and get his gun up but the smaller Haunted had already begun to move.

It dove headfirst over the counter, and into Nick sending him flying into Tom and me. We crashed backwards to the floor, but Nick landed on his shoulder, and managed to use his momentum to roll through the fall, and back up to his feet. The Haunted was sprinting for the hallway leading to the theaters, and Nick was trailing behind trying to steady his aim. He fired twice but was unable to steady his shot on the run. The first shot struck it between the shoulders and the second hit the back of its neck but did nothing to slow it down. As it fled further down the hall Nick followed at a furious pace.

Tom shouted after him but it was useless. He raced after the Haunted with complete abandon, ignoring everything except his target. We hurried after him and I quickly took the lead. The hallways were completely dark and Nick had at least thought enough to turn on his light. The light was unsteady and jumped madly from the Haunted, to the rows of movie posters framed on the walls, down to the dark carpet spotted with odd shapes and colorful designs, and then back up again. Occasionally it would light upon the big wooden doors of one of the many theater rooms we were passing.

The hall came to an end with two halls connecting to the left and right of it. The Haunted continued running full tilt as it neared the end of the hall. When it came to the end it turned sharply to the right, planting its foot on the wall and letting its momentum take it a few steps up making the turn without even breaking its stride. Nick followed with far less grace, but managed to make the turn anyway. I had closed some of the distance on Nick and turned the corner only six steps behind and gaining.

The adrenaline was really pumping at this point and my abilities were beginning to kick in. I still hadn't gotten to the point where I could use them at will. I still needed a rush in adrenaline to jump start them, but I no longer needed rage, which allowed me to maintain my rational thinking. As I rounded the corner I saw that Nick had slowed and steadied his light.

As I slowed to avoid a collision with Nick I could see that the Haunted had vanished from the hallway. This hallway was shorter than the main hallway leading to it, but contained four more theater rooms. They were two to a side, and ended in two big exit doors.

Before I even had time to wonder which door it took I heard the faint thud of a heavy door slowly swinging closed all the way down the hall, and to the left. Nick heard it too and took off like a shot towards it. Luckily I reacted quickly and was still worked up enough to be running at Haunted speed. I caught him a few feet short of the door and yanked him back, pinning him against the wall.

"What are you thinking? Are you stupid?" The words were coming out with more force, and anger than I had intended on using.

Nick started squirming against my grip. "Dude chill out, and get off me! I wasn't going to go all the way in, just take a peek."

I released him and took a step back. "I'm sorry Nick, but we have no idea how many are in there or where. We can't risk it, it sucks but it looks like one just got away."

He looked pretty crestfallen but reluctantly agreed. He brightened up when he saw Tom down the hall. Seeing that we were okay Tom had abandoned running and was walking to us at a leisurely pace and breathing heavily. Nick couldn't help mocking him. "I almost forgot about you. Did you stop at the snack bar on the way?"

Between breaths Tom managed to huff out his response. "Shut up. What were you- Why did you- I hate you."

Nick laughed, and started walking towards his uncle. I lagged behind, still trying to get my adrenaline rush under control, when I caught sight of something in my peripheral. I had ended up almost directly in front of the door of the room that Nick nearly chased the Haunted into but my eye had picked up movement from the door on the other side.

As I turned and saw the Haunted hurtling through the air at me I had no time to react, only enough time to register three quick thoughts. The first was that this was the Haunted we had been chasing. The second was that because this was the Haunted we had been chasing, that meant it had set a trap by pulling the door on the left open while it hid behind the door on the right. The third was wondering how I could be stupid enough to fall for it. It crashed into me and sent us both through the door behind me.

As we hit the ground I managed to transfer the momentum into a throw by letting myself roll backwards, grabbing it by the arms, and pushing up while applying a kick with my left leg. The awkward maneuver managed to throw it clear of me.

For a split second I wanted to attack, but in the dark room visibility was zero, and I knew we were being watched. I couldn't see anything, but somehow I could feel the gazes of the Haunted in that room and knew that we had just gotten their attention. I barreled out of there and nearly bowled Tom over in the process.

They'd both been on their way to come help me, and they both started asking me questions at the same time, but the panic in my voice shut them both up instantly. "We have to get out now!" I turned towards the exit doors at the end of the hall but before I could move any further the Haunted was flying through the doorway looking ready for round two.

This time I was able to get my hands up in a defensive posture. It slammed me against the wall by my shoulders and tried to wrap its hands around my throat. It was practically snarling as hate, and saliva, seethed from its face. It tried to crush my throat, but I had kept my forearms tucked in a blocking posture front of my face, and was able to knock its arms wide by opening up my guard. I then unleashed a rapid succession of blows to its body that forced it back a few steps.

As I began to advance towards the stumbling Haunted to press my momentary advantage I heard Tom bellow "Get out of the way!"

I fell back against the wall as Tom moved in and fired a near point blank shotgun blast to its head, leaving almost nothing in its place. The force of the shot flung the body wildly backwards, flailing like a marionette into the exit door. The door flung open as the body fell limply to the ground halfway past the threshold. Cold air swept into the corridor as the night beckoned to us from just beyond our reach. It was so close and yet so far as they say. More Haunted had already begun to pile into the hallway and our escape was quickly blocked off. The ruckus drew the attention of the Haunted in the opposite theater as well, and pretty soon the hall was choked with them as we fled the scene in a panicked run.

Tom emptied his remaining eight shells while running backwards then turned, dropped the shotgun and ran at a speed that was downright shocking for a man his size. He had kept his shots low on purpose, choosing to shoot their legs and trip them up rather than trying for any kill shots. His tactic caused the Haunted who had been hit to fall and get tangled in the legs of the Haunted behind. This caused a bit of a pile up as the Haunted in the back had to climb over the giant mass of tangled bodies. The delay was not nearly as long as we would have liked however, as we still had several Haunted right on our tails.

I was faster than either Tom or Nick at this point, but deliberately slowed myself to their speed, and put a hand on both their backs to gently encourage them to run faster. Tom was huffing and puffing, and screaming into his walkie talkie as we made it out of the hallway, and sprinted for the door. When we reached the doors I took the lead and shoulder blocked the door open.

We burst through the door into a flood of flashlight beams and once we were a few paces clear of the door we heard Mark's voice booming out a single command. "Get on the ground now!"

Luckily for us when Nick first took off after the smaller Haunted in the theater Tom got on the radio and updated Mark who called everyone back to the front in case we needed backup. When Tom started screaming that we were heading to the front with an entourage they set up a firing squad, took aim on the front doors, and prepared to light up the night.

We were moving pretty fast when we hit the deck and didn't have enough time to have a soft landing, but at that point a few scrapes and bruises were the least of our worries. The report from the rifles broke over us like a tidal wave of sound, and broken glass and warm blood sprayed us like an ocean mist.

It seemed like the gunfire went on forever as we lay pinned down hoping our teammates could stem the rising tide of Haunted flowing through the theater doors. Abruptly the onslaught of gunfire ended. The silence seemed louder than the noise had been, and my ears were still ringing when I saw Mark motioning us forward. The words he was yelling at us were just dull noise, but his wild gestures made it obvious that it was running time again.

They started reloading as we ran to join them. The front doors to the theater had served as a choke point, and it took a few moments for more Haunted to claw their way through the wall of bodies. We started falling back while Mark got on the radio and told Wes and Alfie to be expecting us. Alfie radioed back with a worried tone. "Is everything okay down there boss?"

"We're having a little more success flushing these things out than we would like. We're falling back to your position. We need to get out of Dodge pretty quick."

"Uhh boss, we are actually heading your way, and we're not alone. Whatever you guys were doing down there made a lot of noise, and attracted some very unwanted attention."

"How much attention?"

"A lot."

Just then we saw the headlights from the two vehicles turn down the road, and come streaking towards the empty parking lot that we were currently retreating into. The vehicles were followed by a surging current of shadows as a flood of Haunted poured across the road faintly silhouetted by the vanishing light.

All but a small burst of light had disappeared behind the horizon, and the sky had turned a darker blue as starlight began to stab through the night sky. Mason and Jonathan turned their sights towards Wes and Alfie, attempting to thin the crowd as much as possible before they made it to us. The moon was bright that night, and provided some illumination, but it was still low light, and a large amount of Haunted so they were barely able to dent the mass.

The rest of us were focused on the Haunted still trickling from the theater, and kept firing on the entrance as we fled further into the parking lot. When we reached Mason and Jonathan's sniper perch they joined us. We began a full fledge run towards Wes and Alfie who had entered at the front entrance to the parking lot. They came to a screeching halt about thirty yards ahead of us. Nick and I were weaponless, and the rest were low on ammo as they unloaded what was left into the advancing mob.

We launched ourselves into the vehicles in a frenzy, attempting to reload, take aim, and fend off the hoard that had us nearly hemmed in. By the time everyone had piled in, the Haunted from the theater had joined the party, so we were now almost completely surrounded. The vehicles lurched forward, and made for the small opening still left between the Haunted. What followed was a blur of gunfire and insane driving, but somehow we came out of it alive.

We were on the freeway and well out of town before anyone said anything. Nick, Tom and I finally had time to breathe, and compute what had just happened. We sat silently as the events replayed in our minds. Mark had also piled into that truck with four others, and he was the first to break the silence. "Tom, please tell me Nick got his first kill at least."

Tom responded quickly, with enough adrenaline still flowing to make his voice sound slightly excited, with an undercurrent of righteous anger. "Yes sir, but you may want to congratulate him quickly. I'm fairly sure I'm going to strangle him to death with my bare hands."

This brought forth raucous laughter from the rest of the group, and broke into a flurry of questions, excited stories, and much more teasing and laughter that went well into the night. I began to realize that as much as I had tried to avoid it, I was fast becoming part of this team.

Thomas Harwick

27

The nightmares are getting worse, and becoming more frequent. They are also beginning to come while I'm awake. It has been almost a week since I have been thrown in here with no food or water. Nothing but this journal, a pen, and the Bible Jacob gave me. Every day I slip closer to the brink, and my deadline is approaching. I am getting ahead of myself though. I guess it is about time to bring you up to date about my current situation. I apologize if it seems rushed, but I run out of time tomorrow.

The trouble began over two weeks ago, which was two weeks since I first joined the merry men. That first mission had acted as an initiation of sorts, and I became more a part of this team with each mission. It seemed like any mission I was involved with found some way of ending up like the first one. It would all seem routine, and then one misstep would snowball until we had an avalanche on our hands. We always seemed to pull through though, and each narrow escape just made me feel that much more a part of them. That's what started my own snowball rolling.

We were having another celebration feast after a successful mission in L.A. We had a very interesting run in with Esau's gang actually, and managed to pull one over on them. Tom and Nick had prepared a mixed bean soup seasoned expertly with chicken bouillon, dried onion, garlic salt, celery seeds, dried parsley, and other spices. It was accompanied by a pasta salad improvised with Ramen, canned black olives, some Italian dressing, and a little parmesan.

Nick and Tom's bickering had been getting worse ever since the disaster that was our first mission, and this night was no different. Tom had asked that Nick be restricted to kitchen duty until he learned to follow orders better, and Mark had agreed. Nick had been impossible since then, and now they were even fighting over the food. Until Tom stopped holding him back Nick had resolved to have no common ground, and managed to pick a fight about anything and everything.

After everyone had eaten, and the group had mostly dispersed to their beds, there were still a few of us hanging around the fire talking. We were down to just myself, Mason, Matt the tech geek, and of course Tom and Nick who were still fighting. We were all laughing at the spectacle as Tom raised his hands in exasperation and, with a very loud exclamation that he was done arguing, sat down to join our conversation. Seeing that he had forced his Uncle's retreat Nick sat down on the opposite side of the circle with a smirk on his face.

The conversation was mostly just the others trying to pry out of me the mysterious reason why I wanted to get to the medical research facility in Phillip's Laboratory. Every few missions they would attempt to pry this information out of me, and so far I had shrugged off and avoided answering their questions.

I had kept this secret when I first arrived only because I had no idea if I could trust them. Now that I was part of the team there wasn't any particular reason that I kept dodging their inquiries except that it just sounded crazy out loud. For whatever reason I finally relented, and told them. I started at Doc and me's first meeting. I continued on through our time with Jacob, Doc's theory about the Sons of Heaven, and our encounter with the Talkers.

When I first mentioned the Sons of Heaven I noticed that Matt's face had gone even paler than usual. He stayed completely silent during the rest of my story. The rest of the group was silent, and listening with rapt attention, especially when I described the Talkers, but Matt's look was much different.

When I had finished he said the one thing I didn't think I would hear that night. "I have heard that name before." His voice was just above a whisper, as if he was talking to himself. When he saw the confused looks on our faces he spoke up. "The Sons of Heaven, I have heard that name before." And so began the avalanche.

Matt started by breaking Mark's rule, and confessing that he was previously a computer hacker which surprised absolutely none of us. He used a lot of tech jargon that flew right over my head, but the gist of it is that he managed to hack into some unnamed high ranking government official's computer. It was while he was digging around for Government conspiracies to leak onto the internet that he stumbled upon a protected file titled only "experiments." He thought it might hold something interesting. It contained the name Sons of Heaven.

He couldn't recall anything else all that interesting in the file. It was mostly medical research that made little to no sense to him. He left the file to search for something a little more conspiratorial, with little success.

Less than an hour later police were knocking down his door and taking him into custody. To his surprise he was taken to a military installation about twenty minutes from the small town he lived in, Edwards Air Force Base.

After hours of being held in a small room of a non-descript building on a military installation without a phone call, or an explanation, Commander Allen entered the room and sat down. He had interrogated Matt for hours trying to determine exactly how much he knew. That was where Matt was when the first Haunted attacks were reported.

Events happened pretty rapidly after that. Troops from the Base were sent to L.A to back up the troops already deployed there. The Haunted were everywhere seemingly overnight. Survivors from the surrounding towns flooded onto the base for protection, and when they began turning most of the personnel on base was lost.

Matt was held during all this time, Constitutional rights were not exactly a huge concern at this point, but his family was part of the survivors who sought shelter on the base. In the end only his youngest brother Jonathan made it alive.

Mark assumed command of the shattered remnant of Edwards Air Force Base. He immediately saw the benefit of having a hacker at his disposal, and switched from unlawfully imprisoning Matt to recruiting him. When he discovered that his kid brother had an almost preternatural ability with a high powered rifle, well that was just icing on the cake. The two brothers had been crucial components to his team ever since.

During Mark's interrogations of Matt he never mentioned the Sons of Heaven. Matt had never figured out what file they thought he had seen, and he didn't much care until he heard me use the same name. It was still too little to go on. We didn't really know anything for sure except that Matt saw a file in a government computer that used the same name as a secret society that Doc's friend had once referenced.

Mark had never brought up a specific file, so it was possible that wasn't even why he was there. Then again, if he was there on behalf of a secret society with ties in the government he probably wouldn't use the name directly anyway. It was all too odd to ignore, but too vague to act on prematurely.

There was a lengthy debate about what we should do with this information, but in the end we decided to keep it to ourselves while we investigated further. Tom thought we owed it to Mark to go straight to him, and give him a chance to explain. The rest of us convinced him that we shouldn't risk tipping our hand too early if there was even the smallest chance that the worst was true. We needed more information plain and simple, and Mason had an idea of how we might get it.

"Well, it's a bit of a long shot, but we could try the Base Command Building. If there are any records of the reason for Mark's visit it would be there. That building still has power, so there is also the very small chance that the file that Matt hacked is in one of those computers."

It all seemed a bit thin, but at least it was a starting point. After a few moments of silence to confirm that no one could come up with a better idea, we got to work planning our mission.

We continued plotting the next day, and decided to make our move the day after that, on a Monday. This was one of the few days that the building was actually used. Every Squad had a leader, and every Monday those leaders gathered for a meeting at the Base Command Building. It was one of the few things that still resembled normal life. Mark would give them the week's schedule for guard duties, and discuss any pressing matters the Squad leaders brought to his attention.

It might seem odd to wait until one of the few days that the building was in use to break into it, but there was some reasoning behind it. Although desk jobs no longer really existed in our world anymore the building was still the office for Mark and several others. During the week there was always a small chance that someone might stop by for an impromptu meeting or some other reason, but by the time the weekly staff meeting was disbursed everyone was too busy to waste any more time in that building.

Mason happened to be the squad leader for the Merry Men, so he was attending the meeting as well. This worked to our advantage. The plan was that after the meeting he would approach Mark with some questions and concerns to lead him away, and keep him occupied. The chances of him coming back after the meeting were as low as everyone else, but he was the one that we couldn't take any chances with.

I can't remember what reason Mason came up with to lure him away, and it doesn't really matter anymore. It worked, we had our chance to comb the files, and we took our time. Thanks to the meetings Mondays were the closest thing we ever got to a day off, so we had a decent window for our search. Tom and Nick wouldn't be needed until dinner time, and I had weaseled out of training with Mike. The search through the files was fruitless, and wasted a couple hours. The next step was to check the computers of which there was no short supply.

The building was very reminiscent of the National Guard building where I had my first experience with Talkers. It was simple and dull colored, but was only a single story building. There was a front reception area filled with cubicles and computers, and a long hallway lined with offices, but this one ended in a conference room.

The conference room was sizeable, with an oak table in the middle that looked as though it could easily seat twenty people. On the right side of the room were two rows of seats on a slightly elevated platform that served as a viewing area for visitors. At the end of the table was a projector, and in front the table was a screen now unused and covered in dust. The wall on the left side of the room was lined with computers on very simple desks.

We started on the computers in the conference room, for no particular reason, but this part was the slowest yet. Matt was the only hacker we had on hand so we had to wait for him to hack into the computers one by one. Once he was in one of us could take over the search, but if any other passwords were encountered Matt was once again required. In the third hour we had made our way to the computers in the offices and we were getting a little restless.

The meetings had started at eight and ended around ten, by the time everyone had cleared and we started our search it was almost eleven. It was now two in the afternoon and we had at least another four hours before Tom and Nick's absence, and the subsequent absence of dinner, would become noticeable. The prospect of another four hours of trudging through Government computers did nothing to ease my restlessness, so I got up to stretch my legs.

This is still taking too long so let me pick up the pace a little. While I was trying to walk out my frustration I noticed that while most of the computers were caked with dust from non use there was one in the corner of the front reception area that was pretty clean.

I asked the others if all the computers they had been encountering had also been dusty, and Matt shot back some comment about the Base not having a proper maid service. Nick quickly chimed in that he was pretty sure his Uncle would have him doing that next, since they were already doing the cooking. This of course ignited another bickering match. When I had managed to break up the fight, and get everyone focused again, we all agreed that it seemed to be the only computer that was fairly clean, and that was pretty weird.

Matt broke in and dug around looking for important files for awhile, and when that was another blank he moved on to the E-mail account. The E-mail account was Mark's and Matt encountered more security than he anticipated. This gave us the impression that we were finally on the right track. What we found was more stunning than we were ready for however, and I'm sorry I can't build to it properly, but we found several communications to someone with a Government E-mail.

His name was Nathan, and the e-mails didn't betray more than that, but they did contain information about the Sons of Heaven. That name was never directly used, but occasionally they would use the terms "The Sons", or "SOH", and refer to "the project". There were E-mails about Mark's interrogations with Matt, and status updates on the Base after the first Haunted attacks. The shocking part though, was that the e-mails continued all the way to the day before our break in.

Matt began to download the e-mails onto a disk so that we could take a closer look later, and we skipped to his most recent e-mail. It was from the sender we now knew only as Nathan. Nathan was informing Mark that his time with what they called "the subject" was nearly at a close.

He told Mark that he understood how invaluable the subject was to his team, and what a powerful ally the subject could be, but that the research team was losing patience. If the subject would not allow testing willingly then he would be made to comply. The research was too important to waste this opportunity.

In the last line Nathan lost the thin veil of coded talk and spoke plainly. "If you think you can get him to join us you better do it quick. I've got a whole lot of pressure being put on me Mark, and I can't buy you any more time. You and you're associate better get him up to that facility before he turns or there will be consequences.

As you can imagine none of us said anything for several moments. Thoughts and scenarios were rocketing through my head so fast that I couldn't organize them. I just stood there trying to process it, and the others didn't quite know what to say to me.

Our stunned silence was intruded upon by the static filled crackle of Matt's radio. He had managed to get away from his radar duties, but he still had to carry a radio in case they needed him, which they apparently did now.

"Hey chief, we are having some major technical difficulties down here."

"What's up guys?"

"We lost the tower near the North Gate."

"What do you mean you lost it?"

"I mean we lost the radar at North Gate. We are getting nothing Chief. We are totally blind on that whole side. I can send someone else, but I don't know how bad the trouble is, and we might end up just having to call you anyway. Plus the security is light on that side today, and I don't think we can afford to be blind for too long."

"Okay it's cool; I'm not that far from North Gate anyway, give me five minutes."

He looked up at us and let out a loud sigh. "Talk about bad timing. Sorry guys, but I gotta go check that out. I'll swing back by and pick you guys up when I'm done."

I answered for Tom and Nick, but without even discussing anything I think we had all come to the same decision. "No need, we are coming with you. It might just be a coincidence but I don't like the timing. Take the disc and we can investigate those e-mails later." With that we headed out, but we never did read those e-mails.

28

I think about that decision now, and I still tell myself it was the right one. It wouldn't have been right to leave him, and sometimes it doesn't matter what you do, some things are just going to happen. I guess I am getting a little ahead of myself again though. The memories are replaying in my head and sometimes it takes me a moment to remember where I am, I need to focus.

Okay, so the downed radar, we went to go fix it, and Matt said it had been tampered with. I don't know exactly what was done to it, but someone had messed it up pretty good. While Matt was buried in the thing Mark radioed asking for an update. Now that I think about it, he didn't sound surprised that I picked up instead of Matt. I guess he was just confirming we were there. It was another half hour before we heard the crash.

Flames erupted from the little guard shack. Tom, Nick, and I stuck our heads out over the rail at the top of the radar tower. Matt asked what in the world that noise was, and we were trying to figure that out ourselves. There was a small pickup truck sticking out of the guard shack, and the bed was alight. It took me a moment or two to realize that the fire was actually a large amount of road flares that had been stuffed upright in a red metal toolbox and lit.

The truck had gone far enough through the shack that the flares had caught the door on fire. The two guards on duty had been outside the shack when it hit, and had to enter the building just to get to the driver. The confused look on their faces when they quickly exited and began looking around the perimeter told me there was no driver. It was truly an odd scene, and before my mind had fully interpreted its meaning I was aware that something had just gone terribly wrong.

Matt said he just needed a few more minutes to get the radar going again, but alarms were going off in the back of my mind. A shadow was creeping across the desert a good mile down the road through the bushes, and Joshua trees.

"Matt, we've got to go, NOW!" The alarm in my voice concerned Tom and Nick, who followed my gaze and displayed the same horror on their faces that I'm sure I had on mine. When Matt asked what the problem was we replied in unison with a single word, "Haunted."

There must have been two hundred of them pouring onto the road and heading straight for us. It suddenly all clicked. The truck was a lure to draw the Haunted, and with no radar no one saw them coming. We got down from that tower like it was on fire, and made our way to Matt's vehicle while Tom screamed our situation into Matt's radio. The guards had the same idea, and were on the way to their vehicle, when we realized we were short a person.

Our panicked shouts were met with Matt's stubborn insistence that he only needed a few more seconds. The Haunted were only a quarter mile away and closing. Despite our protests Matt still refused to budge until he had that radar fixed. The guards were yelling at us to get to our vehicle as they fled to theirs. Tom and I were practically dragging Nick that way. From the top of the tower we heard Matt's joyous proclamation, he had finally got it.

Nick managed to wriggle away from us. As he ran back towards the tower he screamed at the guards calling them cowards, and tried to urge them back towards the tower. One of them said "knock yourself out kid" and tossed him his rifle before both guards jumped in their vehicle and sped away. Matt was halfway down from the tower, and the first wave was on us as Nick ran into its midst opening fire.

Tom and I were trailing just behind Nick, and raised our weapons against the swelling tide of Haunted. We had not begun our day prepared for a firefight, and as such the only weapons I had were my pistol and knife. Tom luckily had brought his shotgun in addition to his sidearm because he didn't like going anywhere without his shotgun.

Nick got off the first shots, and they were actually pretty good ones. One of the Haunted had leapt at the ladder and Nick picked it off in mid flight. He then began firing in short controlled bursts and with surprising accuracy on the other Haunted that were rushing in.

Despite the fact that the Haunted that had leapt at Matt no longer had a head, the momentum carried its limp body into the ladder, and knocked him from it. He fell awkwardly to the ground, and we heard the horrific sound of his leg snapping even through all the noise of our gunfire and the roar of the Haunted.

The Haunted had been running full tilt across the desert, and naturally they began to separate based on speed. This meant that the full numbers didn't hit us right away, and was our only chance. We had to grab Matt and get to the vehicle before the slower Haunted caught up with the group that had rushed in first. We had killed ten or fifteen of them and had a few seconds before the next wave hit.

Nick was trying to drag Matt to the truck when Tom pushed him out of the way, and told him to get to the truck. Nick started to protest and exclaim that he wasn't going to leave Matt behind, but Tom had already started hoisting the hacker onto his shoulders, and replied that he wasn't going to either.

The next wave hit as the big man started lumbering towards our last hope for escape with Matt laying across his shoulders in a fireman's carry. Matt had gone unconscious which was probably for the best, because with every step and every fired shot it became more apparent that we were not going to make it. The third wave hit moments after the second. The mass of Haunted began to pour around, flanking us, and beginning to choke off our escape route.

Nick emptied the rifle, and let it drop to the ground as Tom tossed the Shotgun his way. Nick caught, pumped, and fired the weapon in one fluid movement killing a Haunted that was diving for his uncle. I had emptied my pistol and was down to my knife, the fighting style Mike had taught me, and my abilities of course. I had far better control over my abilities at this point and I was squeezing out every ounce of them that I could muster.

As Tom barreled forward trying to beat the horde to the vehicle Nick downed another two on the left. They tangled under the feet of the Haunted behind them causing a slight pile up. My knife was a blur of metal and blood as I downed two on the right, and clubbed a third in the skull with the butt of my pistol. The side arm exploded into pieces, and stunned the creature long enough for me to finish the job with my knife.

Tom called my name, and without really looking tossed his pistol in my general direction. I caught it with the barrel inches away from the left eye of a Haunted and pulled the trigger.

The hole in front of Tom closed and he let out a loud curse just as a Haunted crashed into him sending Matt rolling into a crowd of them. The Haunted pinned Tom to the ground, and let out a bloodthirsty scream as it pulled its fist back preparing to beat him to death. Nick pulled his trigger, and cursed when he realized he was out of shells. He grabbed the shotgun by the barrel and swung it like a baseball bat into the things head. Chunks of the stock splintered off and the thing rolled off Tom, but it quickly recovered, and came charging into Nick.

He wasn't able to dodge its headfirst dive into him, and the two went skidding a few feet over the pavement. We had gotten slightly separated at this point, and there were a few Haunted between Nick and me. I was desperately trying to hack my way to him when Tom came barreling after the haunted with a primal roar.

The big man laid a terrific shoulder tackle on the beast sending it to the ground and landing on top of it. It reached up to choke him, but he didn't let up. He drove both his thumbs deep into its eye sockets. It screamed horrifically, threw him to the side and rolled to its feet. It stumbled about aimlessly as its eyes began to reform, but by that time I had made it back to them and finished it.

The sea of Haunted was crashing in around us and forcing us back in retreat. We couldn't even tell which way the vehicle was at this point. All we could see was the encroaching mass of Haunted. Matt was dead, we were hemmed in, and the only weapon we had left was my knife. The others moved behind me and I became our sole defense.

Their full numbers were on us, but the Haunted were still attacking only a few at a time. With such a large number of Haunted mobbed together in such a big group many of them were fighting each other. Others were just drawn to the commotion and hadn't pushed through the crowd yet. Some seemed content to just toy with us and wait for an opening.

I poured everything into my attacks, and fought back with increasing ferocity and desperation. My wife, all the friends I'd lost, Mark's betrayal, the Sons of Heaven, our failure to save Matt, my failure to lead us out of this mess, it all bubbled up in me and seeped down into my blade. The actions themselves remain a blur, but I know my abilities reached a whole new level.

My attacks were faster than ever and I was able to predict and react just as fluidly as Mike, but with the strength and speed of a Haunted. No matter how hard I fought back though, I was uselessly thrashing against an unrelenting tide, and I couldn't keep it up forever.

We continued backing up until we realized that we had been pressed back all the way to the pickup truck that was embedded into the guard shack. There was a slight break in the attacks as the Haunted hovered around us in a cloud of sneers, snarls, and twisted grins. Tom started telling me to get Nick to the top of the shack. When I turned to tell him that high ground would do us no good in this situation I saw that he was pulling some of the still lit road flares from the bed of the truck. He turned and calmly but firmly said "I'll distract them, get Nick out of here."

Nick didn't know quite what was going on, but followed me up the truck and onto the shack. After I pulled him up, he turned to help pull his uncle up and saw Tom standing there with road flares in both hands keeping the Haunted focused on him. He realized immediately what was happening, and I was barely able to grab him and keep him from jumping down there. He was screaming and trying to wrench loose from my grip when the first Haunted leapt for Tom.

Tom let himself fall to the ground on his back, the Haunted narrowly missing him, and rolled under the truck. Nick had stopped fighting and stood there frozen in horror as the Haunted crowded around the truck. I scooped Nick up over my shoulder, ran to the end of the roof, and leapt as far as I could. Tom must have found the fuel line or ruptured the tank on the truck, and used the flare to light the gas, because as Nick and I landed hard twenty feet from the Guard shack, thunder erupted through the air.

Flames licked the sky, and debris from the truck flew everywhere. Nick had rolled to a stop several feet from me, and was pulling himself off the ground. I could feel my broken leg beginning to heal. Nick looked like he was about to run back to the flames, but I screamed at him to keep moving, and he forced himself forward.

The explosion didn't do all that much to dwindle the number of Haunted, but it sure got their attention. I knew this wouldn't last forever though, and sure enough some of the stragglers at the outskirts of the horde noticed us scurrying away and gave chase. My leg had healed, and I might have outrun them, but not with Nick. I told him to keep going and turned to resume the fight.

Two of them were tearing towards me with the familiar look of murder in their eyes. The first one had just about reached me when its head sprayed red mist and chunks of skull into the air, and the body fell to the ground like a puppet with the strings cut. The second one got all the way to me, and managed to leap at me before it too filled the air with the contents of its head, and its momentum carried the body past me.

I turned back towards Nick, and saw a Jeep stopped about fifty yards away. There was a man standing in the back with a sniper rifle resting on the roll bar. This I assumed was Jonathan, and behind them I could see several more jeeps speeding towards us. The Calvary had finally showed.

29

There were five jeeps total with just over twenty men, and a small armory worth of weapons. They set up a firing line about twenty feet in front of the Jeep Jonathan was in. Jonathan didn't seem to register any reaction when he found out about Matt, but I could see the darkness creeping across his features. He buried his face behind his scope and the shots rang out in rapid succession.

It didn't seem possible, but he seemed even faster and more accurate than usual. He had brought his favorite rifle with him, a fifty caliber monster that he had traded from an ex-military, survivalist type, at a great cost. He also brought two other rifles, and as soon as he emptied one he handed it off to be reloaded while he moved to the next gun. He was in another world now, pouring his grief into every bullet, just as I had done earlier with my knife.

The fire held the attention of most of the Haunted, while Jonathan picked them off one by one. Whenever some of the Haunted noticed, and headed our way, they ran into a wall of gunfire. Pretty soon we were pressing forward, cleaning up the remnants. Nick and I procured some rifles and rejoined the fight. Nick fought his way to the truck, but the fire was still burning too violently to get very close. He fell to his knees unaware and unconcerned with the fight going on around him. I walked over and put a hand on his shoulder, and just stood there with him as his body began to convulse into sobbing.

The wind had begun to pick up. It blew the sickeningly sweet, putrid smell of burning rubber, plastic, and human flesh. The gunshots were still ringing out, but they seemed to come from another world. Everything was muddled as if the world had been plunged underwater. All that was left was Nick, me, the burial pyre of a truck, and the sorrow.

The insignificant voices of the scene swirled around us calling out orders, demanding answers. One voice came into focus in my mind when I realized whose it was. Lightning shot through my spine, and I made no move to turn around, but my mind was working on overdrive. Mark and Mason had reached the scene.

"Nick. Man, I am so sorry." Mason was behind us now, and though neither one of us made a move, I could see Nick's muscles tensing. The sobbing had stopped instantly, and the grief had begun to leave his face, replaced by a creeping darkness.

Words like anger, hate, and revenge become so inadequate in certain situations. Mason had betrayed us, it was the only explanation. He had deliberately led us into a trap that got Matt killed and cost Nick his Uncle, and now he was offering words of consolation? We don't have words for that, but I guess the best way to describe the look on Nick's face would be complete and utter contempt.

Nick was still kneeling in front of the burning truck with an automatic rifle lying on the ground in front of him. He clenched his fists until his knuckles were bright white. Mark came over and added his sympathies. Nicks fists opened up, and his hands moved smoothly towards the gun in front of him. I was watching him closely, and just as he made his move I gripped his shoulder so hard he winced, and stopped reaching for the gun.

He looked up at me quizzically, and I leaned in close so the other two couldn't hear me. "We can't make a move yet, we need to think this through." He started to pull away with a look of disgust on his face, but I held his arm tighter and forced him to hear me out. "The rest of this Base doesn't know what we know Nick. The next move is ours, and it has to be the right one, or your uncle's sacrifice will be in vain. We'll discuss it later."

I released my grip; he quickly got up, and walked past Mason and Mark, and towards one of the jeeps. As he passed he locked his eyes on Mason, attempting to transfer all his hate through that one stare, and walked on in deafening silence. Mark left soon after as well, after leaving me with words of consolation as weak as the ones he gave to Nick.

Now it was just Mason and I face to face, and I found myself struggling not to raise my gun and shoot him like Nick had wanted to. We stood there staring at each other, each trying to read the other, and decide how much he knew. Mason spoke first.

"What in the world happened? What did you guys find? More importantly, what do we do now?"

"There is no we, and I think you have done enough."

He went through the gamut of facial expressions. First there was confusion, followed by realization and shock. He was faking, but he did such a good job I wondered if he had real emotions at all. "I get it, you think since I wasn't with you guys, and I'm the only other person who knows what we talked about that I have to be the traitor. I understand why you would, but don't you think I would try not to make it look so obvious?"

"Not if you expected us all to die."

"Maybe, but the fact remains that it wasn't me. Mark has spies everywhere. Maybe they overheard us talking or something. Maybe they just thought we were acting suspicious and tailed us, but it wasn't me. You still haven't told me what you found, or how deep Mark is involved. Are you going to expose him?" There it was. He just wanted to know how much more damage control he needed to do.

"Anything we had is gone now, and we never got to look at it, we're done."

"Really, just like that you're giving up? You expect me to believe you'd just let something like this stand?"

"Look, the kid just lost all the family he had left, and I know how that feels, okay? I'm tired of seeing people go through that because they help me. I'm done; answers aren't worth this much suffering. You can tell your boss that I won't be any more trouble." I began to walk away and heard his voice behind me.

"He isn't my boss, and I'm not your enemy Isaac, no matter what you may think."

I made no reply, but just kept walking. Mason was right about one thing. I had no intention of letting this stand, but I needed them to think it was over to keep anyone else from getting hurt. As Sun Tzu would say "All war is deception."

Nick made dinner that night, despite our repeated insistence that we could fend for ourselves. I think he saw it as a tribute to his uncle's memory. When we finally had a chance to speak privately about our next move, I could tell that the anger and hate in Nick that burned so hot towards Mason and Mark had died down, and left only the embers of grief and remorse.

"I'm really sorry about almost losing it with Mason. I should have thought it out better."

"There's nothing to apologize for Nick, no one could be expected to think clearly in that situation. I want to put a bullet in his skull too, but I also want to keep you safe." My words didn't seem to register. He was staring somewhere else and nowhere at the same time, and talking as much to himself as to me.

"That's just how I am. I rush in and I don't even stop to think. If I had just listened to Tom he might still be alive." He hung his head and just sat there drowning in his guilt. I have always been pretty useless in emotional situations like that. I never know the right thing to say, but my heart broke for the kid and I knew I had to try.

I sat down next to him and rested my hand on his shoulder. "I just figured out why I like you so much Nick." He looked up at me confused. I imagine that wasn't on the list of things he thought I would say. "You remind me of my wife. I don't talk about her much, because it's still too hard, but she was a lot like you. When she wanted to do something she tended to rush in like you. When she thought something was the right thing to do, nothing could convince her otherwise."

Nick let a half smile break through. "That does sound like me."

I chuckled a little at the memory. "Man, I used to hate that so much it made my head hurt. Now that she's gone I miss that a lot. She was strong Nick; strong willed, and strong minded. Sometimes it felt like everything was just such a battle with her, but that's one of the things I always loved about her. She was unshakeable. I just wanted to keep her safe, to get her through this you know? She just wouldn't stop trying to help other people no matter the risks. It was maddening, and sometimes foolish, but it was always the right thing to do. That's the thing; there is a big difference between being right, and doing right.

"She had this list she kept of people that we came across who had died, or other survivors that we saw die. She would record who they were and how they died, so that if we made it out we could track down their families and at least provide some closure. We would be moving through the city trying to escape these monsters, and she would stop to search a dead body for identification so that we could tell their family. It was crazy and absurd, and I told her that, but in truth I wouldn't have changed that about her even if I could.

"That's how I know that your Uncle was proud of you when you refused to leave Matt. He wanted to protect you, but deep down he was happy that you would rather do the right thing than the smart thing. He willingly sacrificed himself to protect that, to protect you, because he loved you and quite frankly the world needs people like you for times like this."

"What's the point though? If we're all infected anyway then it's just a matter of time isn't it?"

"Probably, I won't lie to you Nick we probably can't win this fight, but the losers are those who don't even try."

"Nice pep talk coach."

"Ya, sorry, I kind of suck at this. Maybe someone comes up with a cure. Maybe you figure a way to let the world know what's really going on, I don't know. But I feel in my gut that you need to survive as long as possible."

"Okay, I think I can handle that." He smiled weakly, and after a moment of awkward silence continued with a note of uncertainty in his voice.

"Isaac, do you believe in Heaven?"

I won't lie, that question kind of hit me out of left field. It's a pretty natural question after losing someone close to you, but being so unable to answer it to myself; I guess I just never thought I would have to answer that question from someone else. I knew his uncle believed. I probably haven't mentioned it yet but Tom was one more devout Christian that I happened to meet along the way.

He and Chappy often had lengthy theological discussions, and the others would engage them in debates over dinner occasionally more for the fun of it than anything. He didn't seem to have any trouble accepting the reality of Heaven. I tried to think of how he would respond to that question. I wondered what my wife would say, or Jacob, or Chappy, but I knew their words would ring hollow in my mouth. I stammered for a bit I suppose, trying to find the right words.

"I'm probably the wrong guy to ask that kid. You should really talk to Chappy." I let that hang there for a bit, and when I saw that he was still staring at me expectantly I continued. "But if you really want my opinion, honestly Nick I have no idea. I mean I want it to be real, because I want to see my wife again. When I sit and think about it though, I mean really try to see the details, I just can't comprehend it. The more I live though the more I think we are not supposed to. I mean look where comprehending stuff has gotten the world. I guess if we could understand, and study things like Heaven, and God, they probably wouldn't be that great."

"Well, that was a very fancy way of saying you have no idea whatsoever."

I laughed pretty hard at that. "I told you that I was the wrong person to ask. Here's the thing; my wife, and your uncle believed without a shadow of a doubt, and I respect their faith. Even if they were wrong I would still want to live and die with that kind of strength and faith. You should strive to be a man worthy of the sacrifice and faith your uncle had in you, and I'll do the same with my wife. As for Heaven, I guess we will both find out one day."

Nick smiled broadly. "You're right Isaac; you were the wrong person to ask."

"I keep trying to be nice kid, and you just keep throwing it back in my face."

I just sat there shaking my head, and Nick laughed until he could hardly breathe. He was almost his old self again. Unfortunately, we had one more thing to discuss and he wasn't going to like it. I waited until he stopped laughing.

"I'm going to go to the medical facility in Philip's Lab. I need to try to find some evidence connected to them, and hopefully some answers. I don't know if I'll be coming back, so I'm going alone. I need you to make good on your promise to survive Nick."

"So you want me to stay here while you go off alone to possibly die? Seriously?" His countenance had fallen again, and we both stayed silent for a time. I felt for him. The situation and the timing sucked, but we needed answers as fast as possible. I didn't trust myself once I got around the people who had created the science that killed my wife, and I didn't want Nick anywhere near me when I turned. When the silence had stretched long enough that I knew Nick had resigned himself to my plan I continued.

"I'll hang around for a few more days to make sure Mason and Mark believe that I've given up. When I leave, if I don't come back soon I want you to get out of here. We still don't know exactly what their agenda is, but I think the farther you can get from this base the better."

The rest of the night was spent in debate. Nick felt that the rest of the Merry Men deserved to know the truth about Mark and Mason, and that Jonathan deserved to know why his brother died. I cautioned him that we had no way of knowing who the rest of the group would be loyal to, and we still had no actual evidence.

I also thought that telling Jonathan about his brother was a mistake. There was no way we could predict or control his reaction. This answer, of course, did not go over well with Nick, who obviously related to Jonathan's situation. Eventually I relented and told Nick I would leave it up to his discretion whether or not to tell the others, but begged him to use his head.

The next three days went by excruciatingly slow as I anticipated my next move, and stayed wary of Mark and Mason. Nick was quiet and almost introspective during those next three days. He took Tom's spot as the cook. This kept him from going on any more missions that might be setups, without it seeming like suspicious behavior.

He spent most of his off time talking to me. We talked mostly about my wife and his uncle, but also about other people we had lost along the way. He also began talking to Chappy more and more. I don't know what's going to happen to all of us stuck in this hell, but for some reason I have this feeling that Nick will make it. As for me, well, I guess it's finally time for that part.

30

We decided that I would leave in the early morning while it was still dark. Nick and I managed to commandeer a vehicle to take us to the facility, since Philip's lab had been situated up in the hills on the North side of the base. We stopped at a bend about a mile from the facility, and out of the sight of any guards. I got out of the vehicle to go the rest of the way alone and on foot. First I made sure that Nick headed back towards camp to replace the stolen vehicle, and wait for me to come back.

The road I was on curved around a steep hill, and I decided to avoid detection by going up and over the hill instead of taking the road. It was still pretty dark out, but the moon was bright that night so I had some measure of visibility. The terrain was made up of flat ruddy looking rocks that looked like broken pieces of pottery littering the ground.

They were very loose, and quite noisy when kicked, preventing me from proceeding with any amount of speed. I didn't think there was much chance of anyone being close enough to hear me kicking rocks around, but since I didn't know where the guards patrolled, I decided to play it safe.

Lizards flitted about the rocks in my wake, making me think more than once that someone had snuck up behind me. No security ever presented itself though, and there appeared to be no one out at this time except me and the lizards.

The horizon was turning a paler shade of blue, without a cloud in the sky, as I stealthily crept to the crest of the hill. The sun had not yet begun its climb of the mist covered mountains in the distance, but it was getting close enough that I was quickly losing my cover of darkness. I picked up the pace a bit.

Halfway down the hill I stopped to survey the facility, and my heart sank. Standing there with a pair of binoculars, watching my descent, was Mark. When he saw I was looking his direction he waved at me, and signaled me to come down. Of all the things for him to do, to just casually wave at me as I was attempting my infiltration, it was thoroughly embarrassing.

I admit my plan was not exactly foolproof up to this point, and to be honest it wasn't really much of a plan. I was hoping to use the early morning darkness to get close enough to their security to survey and play it by ear. Now I was just completely thrown, my only option seemed to be to just openly confront Mark at the front gate.

He appeared to be alone. My eyes were darting around trying to spot guards waiting to take me down, but if anyone was hiding they were doing a remarkable job of it. He knew that I knew about him. What I didn't know was why he would show up alone. Why risk a confrontation with someone who has the physical abilities of a Haunted, and a pretty massive chip on their shoulder concerning you killing their friends?

He was hopelessly outmatched, and that scared me most of all. I haven't had the time to present Mark as completely as I would have liked to. I respected that man as a leader, and even as a friend. That was what made his betrayal so gut wrenching, and I only knew him three weeks. I say all that to say this; if there was one thing I knew about Mark it was that he would never initiate a confrontation unless he held the upper hand. There was something I was missing, I just couldn't see it.

I decided that the best move was to just play along and let Mark make the first move. As I approached he smiled broadly like he was greeting an old friend that he had run into unexpectedly, but there was something new and sinister to that smile.

"Well, fancy meeting you here." His voice was cold and emotionless, or maybe it just seemed that way.

"Something tells me this is more than just a chance encounter." Something deep inside me wanted to just reach out, and strangle him while I still had the chance, but something else told me I needed to wait for the whole picture. Both feelings were probably correct, but I chose to wait.

"Well, if we dance around this we'll be out here all day, let's put our cards on the table. Tell me what you've figured out, and I can fill in the rest."

"That easy? You'll just give me all the answers?"

"It would save time."

I decided to play along. "I know about the Sons of Heaven, and that you're part of them. They've infiltrated at least parts of our government. You are reporting to a man named Nathan, and he wants you to deliver me here. I saved you the trouble, so you're welcome. Last, but most definitely not least, I know that when you're little lackey told you we were close to the truth you had him set a trap that got two good men killed."

Mark smiled weakly. He began looking less sinister and more exhausted than anything. "Well, you know more than I would have guessed, but I'm afraid you're still misinformed. Mason is far from my lackey, and he forced our hand by sending you to my office. I doubt you will believe me, but I never wanted anyone to die over this."

"Save your breath, I don't. What's to stop me from killing you right here?"

He casually handed me the binoculars, and pointed to a cluster of tumble weeds about halfway up the hill's slope. There was a figure creeping slowly towards it, and using it for cover. I let out a heavy sigh and shook my head in frustration. "You've got to be kidding me. Kid, why can't you just listen?"

Light had begun its takeover of the skies, but it was still dark enough that I could only make out the form of someone crouching behind the dead looking sage brush, and not the actual details. Not that it mattered really, I knew who it was.

"He's not one for taking orders is he? I know you feel responsible for him now, and I respect that. You don't have to protect him from me. I don't want to hurt him, or anyone else, but I will if you force my hand. Take a look at that group of large rocks about twenty feet down from the crest of the hill."

I looked where he told me to. Hiding behind the rocks, staring down the scope of his rifle at Nick, was Mason. "Leave the kid out of this." It was a simple enough statement, but I said it with murder in my eyes and rage in my veins. If they killed the kid I would have ripped Mark limb from limb, and I think he saw that.

He smiled and gestured towards the door. "Nobody has to get hurt here. I just want to go inside and have a calm, peaceful, chat. I assume you told him to go back to camp, and wait for you to come back before making any rash decisions." I nodded my head. "And he pretended to leave, and tailed you instead. That definitely sounds like Nick. He's getting sent back, that part is certain. I'll let you choose if he's breathing at the end of it." He gestured towards the door.

So there was Mark's ace in the hole. I might have tried to kill him if only my life was in the balance, but I couldn't risk it with Nick. I wouldn't risk it with Nick. I nodded, waited until he had called off Mason, and walked into his trap.

31

I would love to give you a description of the interior of the facility once known as Philip's Laboratory, but I didn't have much of a chance to take in the sights. Just a few steps after entering that doorway I heard the door close, and felt a sudden stabbing pain as Mark slammed a syringe in my neck, and injected its contents before I realized what was happening. I swung around wildly after the attack, but as I stopped to face Mark the room kept going. The air thickened to the consistency of pancake batter, and I stumbled forward a step before the floor reached up and punched me in the face.

When I woke up I was in a cell of sorts. It's a little hard to explain. I think it used to be an office judging by the carpet that was left, and the fact the hallway looked like the same setup as the other office buildings on the base. There had definitely been some remodeling going on though. The walls had been knocked down and rebuilt in concrete, and the front of the room appeared to be Plexiglas, even the door. There was a small slot for speaking. It was slid open.

The room was empty except for a small cot which I was laying in, and some blankets that were folded and lying neatly in the corner. The two rooms on the other side of the hall were the same way, minus the cot and blankets.

Outside my strange cell Mark was sitting in an office chair, rocking back and forth, whistling. I sat up slowly, trying to pull my brain out of the dense fog and into the aching clarity of consciousness. The lights overhead burned with intensity, and the room came into a sharper focus than I thought the human eye capable of capturing. I may be exaggerating slightly of course, but phrases like "my head ached" and "my eyes hurt" just don't convey the agony I was in properly.

When I stood up I supported myself against the wall with my right hand, and used my left to massage my eyes until they didn't feel like someone was using them as pin cushions. Mark took notice of my struggles and came to his feet with an unsettling smile. "Well, look whose back in the land of the living. Did you enjoy your nap?"

I was still too woozy to get very worked up; instead I just mumbled a series of questions. "How long have I been out? What did you do to me? How did you... where are we?"

He laughed a little at my dazed stupor. "Well, let me take those in order. You've been unconscious all of fifteen minutes. I tranquilized you using a little custom recipe the geeks here in the lab have cooked up for Haunted. Did you know you could be tranquilized? We've been doing some testing on you during your "routine examinations", and on some Haunted we have managed to capture and detain here.

"Turns out that since our little sleepy time formula doesn't destroy any cells, your ability to fight illness doesn't apply. However, you do burn through it at a greatly increased rate, so we have to hit you with a dose that could stop a rhino in its tracks. Even then we only get about fifteen minutes, interesting isn't it?"

"As informational as that all is those aren't the facts I was hoping to dig up. I don't know what you hoped to accomplish with that little stunt, but if you don't start giving me those answers you promised I'm going to go to plan B."

"And what exactly is plan B?"

I leaned closer until my mouth was right next to the slot. "Kill you and let the chips fall where they may."

"There is a little flaw in your plan there Isaac, that isn't exactly a cardboard box that you are sitting in. These rooms are specifically designed for holding Haunted; those concrete walls are three feet thick." He rapped his knuckles against the glass a couple of times.

"This is three inch thick ballistic glass, and if you somehow did get out, there are several guards at the end of that hall that are itching for some target practice. Oddly enough, none of that is what will hold you in that cell. I am going to give you your answers, and then provide you with a scenario and a choice. I think that choice will hold you in there better than any fortification we can make. But first, I will tell you the truth about what's been going on here."

"I'll give you the condensed version, and it will likely sound insane, but revolutionary things usually do. I am part of the Sons of Heaven, as you already knew. We are a secret society of sorts, and as you guessed we have infiltrated several levels of the Government. Not just the United States, this society extends to all corners of the globe. We are behind the treatment that created the Haunted, and the virus that caused the need for the treatment. We knew all along what the treatment could do. Immortality was always the goal, but the Haunted was not. That was merely the lemons for our lemonade as it were."

"It was just a happy little accident? You destroyed millions of lives and you're looking for a silver lining?"

"Those lives have been destroyed all along, they just didn't realize it. It may look cruel to you, but we're trying to build a new world. We are restoring purpose to purposeless existence. That can't be done without grave sacrifices. We need to bring the world to its knees, and make governments beg us to save them. The virus was the plan, but I think you will agree that the Haunted are so much more terrifying."

"You're right, it does sound insane. Do you even hear yourself? Who gave you the right to decide that our lives are necessary sacrifices?"

"Well, honestly I don't. I am afraid I am lower on the totem pole than you would like, but I still know enough of the mission to give you some answers."

"So, what are you then, middle management?"

"More like security detail. Originally I came to interrogate Matt and find out how much he knew. It was decided that I would stay during the test to protect the research facility here. I was also the driving force behind the quarantine and the restriction of communication.

"I also help the geeks catch some live Haunted to test from time to time. When you came along they wanted to test on you right away, but I saw the potential weapon you could be. There's something about you Isaac. You have been able to channel your abilities like no one else I've seen. When you got to the point that you could bring on your abilities without being enraged they started to see it too." He let out a short chuckle. "When you made it to week three without giving in to the next stage I thought their heads were going to explode."

"Well maybe I can help them with that. So, if you are the researcher's babysitter and go-for, then what is Mason, your henchman?"

"I told you before you were wrong about that. Mason is the money, or at least part of it. Some of us are part of the Sons because of our position, or our ability, and some are in because revolutions are not cheap. It might surprise you to learn that Mason is actually a multi-millionaire. I can see by your expression it does. Mason's father was a very wealthy weapons designer and Mason his only child. He died a few years ago leaving Mason his entire fortune.

"Mason has contributed a tremendous amount of money for his spot in the organization. Not to mention resources and technology from his father's company. He probably carries more clout in the actual organization than I do honestly. I have been given command, but he enjoys forcing my hand. He can be pretty hard to work with sometimes to be frank."

"I understand why they would need you, and apparently Mason moneybags, but what exactly are you two getting out of this? Are you just doing their dirty work so you don't have to be a sacrifice for this 'new world' of theirs?"

"Please don't misunderstand my intentions, or motivation. I don't intend to be a part of that world. It's not for me. I want to be part of making a better world for future generations who won't know what we've known, or see what we've seen. No more hate, deceit, or war, just peace. I believe in their dream, but there is no place for an old soldier like me in that world. This is my new world, or rather my last stand.

"I have grown so tired of the politics, the paperwork, the smiling and hand shaking. I'm weary of sucking up to idiot politicians, and sitting on the sidelines. I wanted to have my final taste of battle. This is my last chance to be a warrior. Not against a bunch of guys with towels on their heads, hiding in caves, and wielding inferior firepower either. I'm on the frontlines of a battle against the greatest threat the world has ever known. This is my Alamo. I don't need immortality, this is more than enough. You would have to ask Mason for his reason, but I'm sure it would have something to do with getting to experience a real zombie apocalypse."

"You are completely insane. All of this so you could die like a warrior? You're a madman who just condoned, and had a hand in, the murder of millions of innocent people."

"There are no innocent people don't you get it?" The sudden loss of composure caught me off guard. Mark had a possessed look in his eyes. "We talk about things like innocence, and freedom, and peace like they are things that still exist in our world, but they don't. If you knew what I know maybe you would see it. We are corrupt to the core. Our leaders are corrupt, and our people are either too naïve, too stupid, or too lazy to do anything about it. We are too far gone to change with anything less than a complete revolution."

"You don't actually intend to overthrow the government do you?"

"Of course not, unfortunately the time of government overthrow is long gone. We are doing the only thing left to do, destroy this world and build a better one."

"Destroy the world?" The words just hung there in front of me. I couldn't believe what I had just heard, and he said it as nonchalantly as if we had been discussing the weather.

"That's what this has all been for. This is the test, and it is going wonderfully. The corporation will wait until the survivors have been whittled down to nothing to release the cure to the Haunted disease and become heroes. The next time the virus is released the whole world will turn to the heroes that saved them from the last outbreak. They will receive the tainted treatment."

"The whole world will become Haunted, and the Sons will hold the only cure. Any government that wants to save themselves will surrender to the Sons of Heaven. They are going to rebuild the world as we know it. They will choose the best of this world, and let the rest die."

"The 'rest' won't go down without a fight."

"That's why you are so important to this plan. We need to study you, and figure out why the treatment failed. If they can perfect it they will be immortal, and no one will stop them."

"You guys are right out of a bad Sci-fi flick, you know that right? Do you really expect me to go along with this? Is that the offer you think will keep me here? If you're counting on my help in developing the cure I'm afraid you're going to be disappointed."

"We already have the cure. It's the answer to what caused the Haunted that we need."

"You already have the cure? Then why aren't you using it?"

"You don't listen very well. We are waiting for most of the population to die out. We want the world to be truly terrified when the 'Virus' comes back, and we don't want too many survivors talking about what happened here. We want the rest of the world to know little about the Haunted until we bring them back. Besides, it really just neutralizes the treatment, and keeps it from reformatting cells.

"At this point the cure will only work in those that haven't heard the call yet; anyone past that point just dies. They still haven't figured that out yet, which is part of why they need your cooperation. They think they have a chance of curing you Isaac."

"How long have you had a cure?" I shouted the question. All I could think about now was Rebecca, and that I might have been able to save her after all.

He continued calmly, unaffected by my emotional outburst. "After the first wave of Haunted on the base we lost most of our personnel. It was after we had replenished our personnel with civilians. I was able to get the cure into the new team before anyone heard the call. I am sure eventually people will start wondering why no one on the base has turned in so long, but so far no one has suspected anything."

He seemed to find my confused look amusing, and smiled slightly as he continued. "Obviously that one caught you off guard. It is just part of my deal. I get my own group of unaffected survivors to help me kill as many Haunted as possible before the end."

"What do you mean the end?"

"Well, they call them last stands for a reason Isaac. I intend to keep taking on the Haunted until they finally get the best of us."

"You're going to lead everyone who follows you to their deaths."

"Eventually, but not immediately, they will have a better chance than most. If you cooperate with us, you can hand pick a small group to take off this base."

"And if I don't cooperate?"

"Then things stay mostly the same. No one makes it out alive, and you die here an unwilling lab rat."

"And if I decide to make my own option?"

"You can't win Isaac, not this time. You could kill me, and it wouldn't change anything. I need you to think about something Isaac. I am a General, I have the clout to order a block of all communications out of the quarantine zone, and control what information gets leaked to the media, and I am lower rung. We have members in every level of every

Government in every country. We won a long time ago, and this is nothing but the endgame."

"I refuse to believe that."

"Well, luckily Isaac, you don't have to believe me to make it the truth. You will see in due time. But I do have an offer to make you, and even though you probably won't believe this, I truly hope you take it. After all I have told you I'm sure you think I don't care about my team, but I do, and you are a part of that team. If you cooperate with the researchers and allow them to run tests on you they are confident that they can find a way to keep you from turning. You would then be welcome to rejoin my team."

"What?"

"I don't let emotions influence my decisions, and you shouldn't either. Let them study you, and they can cure you, and then you can make a decision. If you choose to come back to my little team then this never happened, and you stay to give them their best chance of survival. You say nothing about what has transpired here, and maybe I can fix it so you have a chance to get them through this alive. If you don't want to rejoin my team, then you can take the kid and a few others, and get off my base, but only after we're done here."

"I won't help you, and I won't let you kill anyone. I'm going to stop you."

"There is no need to make that decision right now. I am going to leave you here to think about my offer. Take some time to think, pray, write in your journal, do whatever it is you need to do. At the end of the week I'll be back to hear your answer, and I hope it is the right one Isaac I really do."

32

So here we are. We have finally arrived at the end of my sad little tale. It may seem a bit anticlimactic to end the story with the hero locked in cage, but I am no hero, and there are no happy endings. It isn't a satisfying close, but I'm afraid this is where my story ends. The week is almost up, and my decision is looming before me.

They think this cage of theirs can hold me, but I can get out any time and have been able to for the last few days. All that has been holding me in this prison has been the desire to finish this account before I turn, and the choice I have to make.

I won't join them. There has never been a doubt in my mind about that. I don't want to abandon my friends. I want to warn them about what is happening and try to save them, but my time is short, and I don't want to miss this opportunity. I can feel the madness creeping slowly over me like extending shadows in the noonday sun. I don't know how much longer I can fight this off. I slip easily in and out of reality now, and the only thing that helps me hold on is this journal, and my choice.

All I am left with is this decision that has been looming in front of me, and holding me here. I could attempt to escape. Get Nick, and whoever else wants to flee the base, to safety somewhere they have a chance to live through this thing. If they get out alive maybe they can find a way to stop the Sons of Heaven's plans, or at least make them public.

I want desperately to help my friends escape, and then meet my death without fear or regret, but that scenario leaves Mark and the rest of them unpunished. After everything they've done, the lives they have toyed with, the numerous hours they spent watching and studying us as we suffered, and all in the name of making the world better. I just can't let that stand.

I'm sorry Rebecca. I wish I was a stronger man, but I don't think I can stop until they see the consequences of their actions. Until they pay for what they did.

No matter what happens next I am afraid this is where I leave you. It is unlikely anyone will ever read this. It is even more unlikely that anyone reading this will be able to do anything to stop the coming events. You now have the truth, and honestly I don't care what you do with it. I leave you to your fate as I go to meet mine.

God, if you are real, if there really is a Heaven, if I really can see Rebecca again. If there is a better way… Please God, stop me.

To Whom It May Concern

My name is Rebecca, and I am a survivor of what we are referring to as the Haunting. Since communications from inside our quarantine zone have been blocked I am assuming that anyone outside has little information about what has been happening.

The world has gone mad in a way I can't begin to explain. I don't think many of us are going to make it out alive so many have already died. That is the purpose of this list. I imagine the only thing worse than hearing that someone you love has died here is not knowing, and with communications blocked I doubt you will find out any other way.

I am sorry that death is the only news I am able to give you, but it's the only consolation I can offer.

The following is a list of people who have died during the quarantine. Some of the names are people my husband and I have met along the way, and some complete strangers. Some of the deaths were witnessed, while others were people we found already dead. I've tried to include age and circumstances of death where I could.

The following names are those who died in the Los Angeles Air Force Base Massacre.

Becky Neese, 58

Vickie Davis Hurst, 89

Lois Burchett Ochu-eberhardt, 59

Patricia Stack Bradley, 56

Harmony Szilagyi, 32

Sean Szilagyi, 28 – Died trying to draw the Haunted away from his wife, but there were just too many.

Dagmar Haskew, 45

Kathy Harwick Foster, 55

Maryah, Travis Stevens – A husband and wife from Pennsylvania who were vacationing here when the virus first hit, and got caught in the Quarantine.

Cory D Mucci, 20 – A bright young man who traveled with us for a few days. He is the first person I have seen turn. It happened so fast. My husband killed him before he hurt anyone.

Trille Jessen, 21 – Poor Trille was unable to deal with the madness any more. I'm not sure why, but when a group of survivors we were traveling with were pinned down and hiding from a group of three Haunted, she removed all of her clothing, screamed that she just wanted it to be over, and ran naked through the street. She lost her mind, but she also distracted the Haunted and saved all of our lives.

Livingston Timsuren, 25 – We traveled with Livingston's family for a while. They happened upon us when we were hungry and short on supplies with nothing to trade the gangs for food. Livingston's family took us in and fed us from their supplies. We were rummaging through some abandoned housing for supplies when a Haunted surprised us, and tackled my husband. Livingston was a cage fighter before the Haunting, and he pulled the Haunted off Isaac, and fought it bare handed. By the time we found a weapon, and managed to kill it Livingston was already dead.

Darin Elliot, 38 – Found bleeding to death in the backyard of his house, presumably killed by looters who ransacked the home. He asked if his family made it, and then passed out from blood loss. He never regained consciousness. It was discovered through search of the house that he had a wife and young daughter, but they were not found in the house or immediate area.

Brittany Cagle, 13 – We found Brittany in the house next door in an empty fridge, holding a baseball bat. I don't know if she was hiding from the Haunted, or the looters. The refrigerator was perforated with bullet holes, whether it was intentional or crossfire I couldn't tell. It didn't matter for poor Brittany, who was hit by several of those shots.

Janice Masei, 44 – When a gunfight broke out between two gangs over supplies Janice shielded a young bystander and was shot to death.

Kirsten Kerkhof, 36 – Died in the crossfire of same gunfight

Jason Lewis, 35 – Drank himself into a stupor and confronted a Haunted head on screaming that they couldn't kill him because he was the devil.

Jeffrey Peterson, 40 – found dying, presumably after a run in with a biker gang. Last words were "I never should have come back to L.A. I hate bikers." His wife Margaret Peterson was found dead next to him.

Renee Aldridge, 50 – Shop owner who refused to turn over her supplies to one of the gangs. She threw coffee in the leaders face and was dragged outside and publically executed.

Kyle Omler – Owned the shop next door and confronted the Gang leader. Was shot in the face multiple times out of annoyance for debating every little thing, such as whether or not the Haunted could actually be classified as zombies.

Shawn Belanger, 40 – Found outside a sports bar holding a broken pool cue that he had lodged into the eye socket of a Haunted wearing an Ohio State Football jersey. Another Haunted apparently snapped his neck while he was busy killing the one in the Ohio State jersey. Shawn was wearing a Michigan football jersey at the time. My husband found this deeply significant.

Juana Maria, age unknown – Juana had come up from Mexico to visit family when the Haunting took place. She joined our group after finding her family butchered by the Haunted. She died in the crossfire of a shoot out between our group, and one of the Latin gangs after she slapped the leader for making advances on her, comparing her to a famous Latin actress. The leader was also shot, and killed.

My name is Isaac. My wife Rebecca will not be able to finish this list. She turned a week ago, and was selfless to the end. I am completely lost without her, and even though I always thought this list was a fool's errand I find myself compelled to finish it. Rebecca believed in this list, and refused to abandon it. Her stubbornness when she was doing what she felt was right was both her most frustrating, and most impressive trait. I will finish her list and get it out of this God forsaken place no matter what. Whoever ends up reading this please know that it was my wife who made it possible.

The following are members of Jacob's group of Christians that entered L.A on a regular basis to collect supplies and escort survivors. Jacob was a Christian, a biker, a great man, and my friend. He was also the twin brother of the leader of one of the more prominent Biker Gangs which allowed him access to the highway system at a much better rate. The brothers weren't on the best of terms but they worked out a deal that let Jacob pay the cost of many survivors and get them out of the city. The following people were lost while distributing and collecting supplies for the churches of Lancaster and Palmdale, and helping to escort myself and others out of the city.

Louanne Page, 40
Jennifer Condon, 28
Tracey Gilmore, 40
Marty Cichowski, 64
Anne Bates, 57

The following names were members of Jacob's group who died in the Haunted attack on the National Guard Armory in East Palmdale. While our small group fought a Talker inside, the rest took on waves of Haunted, and two more Talkers outside. They fought bravely, and died tragically, and I will never forget their sacrifice. They died during my search for answers, and I can't help feeling responsible. I only hope that their beliefs were founded, and they have found the life in death that they were promised.

Rebecca Harwick

Don Harwick
Sarah White
Becky Wheeler-Mccartin
Dana Fritz
Carrissa Hanes
Joe Davenport

The following names were collected during my missions with the Merry Men, an unusual group of survivors that held Edwards AFB, and actively tracked and killed Haunted in the surrounding areas. Most of the deceased were found in the cities of Lancaster, and Palmdale.

Ricarda Tesch, 23 – German citizen, presumably a tourist, she was found beaten to death in the store room of a café clutching a fantasy novel.

Sarah Ford, 20 – Killed in the crossfire when a gang made a raid on a firearms store that was being held by a group of ex military survivalists in Lancaster.

Rachel Redmond, 20 – died by self inflicted gunshot next to her friend Sarah Ford

Annette Anderson, 18 and Alexia Michaels, 17 – Shot to death attempting to steal supplies from a gang and left out front of the shopping center they were occupying as a warning

The following were victims of a Haunted attack on an apartment complex. A group of survivors tried to make a last stand against a very large horde of Haunted. Many of the remains were unidentifiable.

Natalie McKay , 28, Kane Caston – Kane was apparently part of the military judging by his dog tag, but the tag was lodged in an exposed vertebra in his neck, and his name was all we could read on it. Both Natalie and Kane were found on the first floor of the building along with many other unidentifiable remains. I believe many of them were corpses of Haunted, these people put up an amazing fight.

Hayden and Christopher Gotz, 16 – Hayden and Chris were twins. Hayden was amazingly still alive when we found him, but not for much longer. He was holding Chris in his arms. Dying words "We were supposed to be on vacation… We weren't supposed to be here."

Kaitlyn Zuver, 18 – Found a short distance from Hayden and Chris, Kaitlyn died from a self inflicted gun wound.

Samantha Jade, 13 – Found dead on stairwell leading to fifth floor. Neck was snapped, presumably by the fall. Don't know if she was pushed, jumped, or just tripped in her panic.

Cam Sparks, 14 – Found dead on stairwell on the eighth floor. There was a pool of blood under Cam stemming from a wound on the back of his head. He was clenching half of a broken pencil in his hand. One of the haunted bodies we found on the eighth floor had the other half of the pencil in its right eye.

Joshua Perry, 21 – Found dead in his hotel room. He was sitting in a chair in front of a small table. His neck was broken, and hanging backwards at an unnatural angle. The table was covered with playing cards.

Natalie Dawn LeBlanc, 26 – Natalie's body was found on the ground outside the complex. It looked like she had fallen from a great height. I originally thought suicide, but she was still clutching a rifle tightly so now I believe she was acting as a lookout, possibly from the roof, and was thrown off by one of the Haunted.

Colleen Ricker, 19 – Colleen managed to survive the Haunted attack on the hotel by hiding in a room on the top floor. Tragically, as we cleared the top floor we entered this room and startled Colleen, who must have mistook us for Haunted, causing her to jump through the window and plummet to her death.

Nichole Bunsen, 25 – Nichole was part of something strange that has been developing during the Haunting. She belonged to a small cult in the city that believes the Haunted are an advanced form of human, a more evolved state that only certain "chosen" people are able to attain. It's their goal to be 'chosen' and survive to become Haunted, thus attaining a higher state of being and greater physical abilities. Nichole walked straight into a group of Haunted with her arms spread, and was torn apart with a smile on her face.

About the Author

Thomas Harwick is a 30 year old Indie Author from the barren wasteland of Southern California's Mojave Desert. His first self-published novel is the sci/fi horror thriller "Sons of Heaven: The Haunted." He is planning release of the sequel "Sons of Heaven: Shadows" in late 2014/ early 2015.

He is also currently working on two mystery novels - "A Shot in the Park" featuring his smart mouthed bounty hunter Archie Dufresne, and an undead caper with his hardboiled sleuth "Cemetery Spade: Zombie Detective"

www.ingramcontent.com/pod-product-compliance
Lightning Source LLC
Chambersburg PA
CBHW070622130626
46556CB00001B/446